A book starts with an idea that becomes an outline that becomes a story,
but a book is never written by one alone.

I would like to thank:
My editor, K.G., for her patience, wonderful talent and encouragement.
My publisher, Dimiter Savoff, Simply Read Books,
for his belief in me and in my stories.
My daughter, Chantel, for her unconditional love and ideas.
My wife, Anita, for her endless, never dwindling support and sunshine.

In memory:
For Martin who stayed true at heart until it broke,
but his light will shine forever.

—O.N.

First published in 2008 by Simply Read Books
www.simplyreadbooks.com

Text © 2008 Oliver Neubert
Cover © 2008 Atanas Atanassov

Cataloguing in Publication Data

Neubert, Oliver, 1961–
Chantel's quest for the golden sword / Oliver Neubert.

ISBN 978-1-894965-81-1

I. Title.

PS8623.E477J32 2008   jC813'.6   C2007-905130-8

We gratefully acknowledge the suppport of the Canada Council of the Arts
and the BC Arts Council for our publishing program.

Book Design by Jacqueline Wang

Printed in Canada   10 9 8 7 6 5 4 3 2 1

Oliver Neubert

CHANTEL'S QUEST
for the Golden Sword

SIMPLY READ BOOKS

WEST

The Four Lands

Table of Contents

CHAPTER ONE

It is Time

The Evil One will return to the four lands
to finish what was started many moon
crossings ago. The destiny of the people will
be in the hands of the Last Descendant, who
will stand against the evil forces. The light
and the dark powers will clash again, and
with it, the pain of the past will return.
Look for the Golden Braid; it is the sign
of the beginning.

From The Book of Erebus

"Wake up! It is time."

Cold mountain air blew into Chantel's bedroom through
an open window. The sun was already peeking into the
green valley, turning the ripples on the blue lake into golden,
dancing stars. Sunbeams illuminated the eight-cornered

tower and filled her room with a warm yellow light.

Chantel did not want to get up. She was very tired. She had woken in the middle of the night because of troubling dreams and saw a strange sight: an eclipse of the blue and red moons. She'd spent a long time gazing out her window at the color-shifting moonlight.

"Wake up!" the voice said again. It was Owl, her guardian.

Chantel yawned and opened her eyes.

Owl was sitting at her desk. His eyes were sapphire blue, his feathers a hundred shades of gray, and his ears abnormally long, with pointed tips.

"Good morning, Owl," Chantel said. "You're up early. Are you finally going to show me how to use my sword?"

"No, not today." Owl's ears twitched nervously. "It's a special day. There are many things we must do."

"Isn't it a bit too early?" Chantel protested, still yawning.

"Today is your twelfth birthday," said Owl. His eyes darted across Chantel's sleepy face and her messy hair.

"My birthday!" Chantel grinned and sat up. "Of course!"

As Owl stared at her hair, he continued, "From this day forward, your life will be changed forever. There . . . there is no easy way for me to tell you this. Please do not be alarmed."

The grin left Chantel's face. Owl was so solemn. Something was obviously wrong.

Owl took a deep breath. Revealing the secret he'd kept faithfully for many years wasn't as easy as he'd imagined. He took another breath and began. "Chantel, you are the protector of all creatures in our four lands. You are the Princess of Freedom."

Chantel blinked. Then she threw herself back onto her

bed and started to laugh. "It's amazing how you can keep a straight face while telling me such a fib, Owl!"

Owl didn't laugh. He sat perfectly still.

"You're serious?" Chantel whispered.

"This may be hard for you to accept, but you must," said Owl. "You are Chantel, Princess of Freedom. You are the one who will free our lands from the Darkness."

The Darkness! Chantel shivered. Owl rarely spoke about the Darkness, but when he did, she always shivered. She didn't know much about the Darkness, except that it was the reason she couldn't leave the castle's grounds, and it had killed her pet, Fawn, a little red fox.

"The Darkness is a force that causes great harm and sadness," continued Owl, "a force that can destroy and hurt. It's in all of us. We have a good side and a dark side within us, but it is up to us to decide which side will prevail.

"There is one creature, however, that has no good side: the Evil One, the one who feels and feeds on the dark side within us. The Evil One is awake again and threatens our four lands. Wild creatures and angry humans are controlling and destroying nature and causing great harm to everyone. Only this castle, cloaked in magic, and a few other places are still safe. But safe and free are two very different things. The world needs someone who can set us free again: you."

"M . . . me? But it can't be me! I don't know anything about the outside world. All I know is this castle and what you've taught me. You must be wrong." Chantel's voice rose in alarm.

Owl shook his head. "Twelve moon crossings ago I received a message. I was sitting in my tree when a golden hummingbird came and said to me, 'Go into the mountains where the waterfall touches the lake. There you will find a child. Protect her, because she is the Princess of Freedom. Mother Nature has rescued her from the evil ones of the four lands. As prophesized, this child is the only hope we have. You must watch over this child until it is time to reveal to her who she is. Take the child to the old castle on the small hill where the boundaries of the four lands meet. There you and she will be safe. No one will be able to see the castle because it is hidden behind a screen of mist. Look after the child and raise her well, because she is our world's only hope.'

"After three days of traveling and searching, I found you lying on a warm patch of green moss. You were only a week old, and you looked at me with such trusting eyes that I fell in love with you right at that moment."

"What about my parents?" Chantel asked.

"All I know is that Mother Nature gave you to me. I love you like you were my own."

"Did Mother Nature take me from my parents?" Chantel wondered aloud. "Or did the Darkness separate us?"

She slowly got out of bed. Owl stayed behind the desk as Chantel stepped into her warm, fluffy house slippers and took her morning coat from the chair at the end of her bed. She walked to one of the tower's windows.

Her bedroom was on the top floor of a large tower that had eight sides. It was part of a small castle built on a low hill. To the north rose majestic mountains; to the east rolled the green forest; to the south lay the golden desert; and to the west a wild ocean beat against a rugged coast.

Chantel looked north towards the tall mountains. Their

spiky peaks were covered with snow, and the waterfall in the distance tumbled down a steep, high cliff. When she looked at the distant mountains and the beautiful green, hilly surroundings, she felt at ease. She was connected to the mountains. She knew it; she felt it, but she was not able to explain it. For the longest time, she had hoped that one day she would find her parents there.

"Princess of Freedom." The words rang in her head. "Mother Nature. A prophecy."

So many questions spun in her mind. She knew she would not find the answers by staring out her window, yet she gazed at the mountains until she felt calm and focused. She had looked at the mountains for many hours after Owl had told her about Fawn's death.

She slowly turned around and looked into Owl's encouraging eyes.

"Please tell me more," she said.

Owl gave a great sigh of relief. She was ready.

"First we eat," he said. "The shadow has reached its midmorning point." With that, Owl flew out of her bedroom.

CHAPTER TWO

The Snow Walker

The Darkness is everywhere, but we cannot see it. It is within us, and only we can control it. It is through our actions, through our thoughts and through our behavior that we show whether we are guided by our good side or misguided by our evil side. We have to decide if we want to take the easy route or to stay true to our beliefs.

From The Book of Erebus

The high mountains of the North were covered with new snow. The Snow Walker came out of his cave into the morning sunshine. Songs of the mountain birds filled the air, and the large snow plateau below him glittered like thousands of little diamonds in the sun's rays. He scowled. He did not care for the pretty songbirds or the beauty that surrounded him.

He stretched. He stood more than seven feet tall. His long black hair was bound in a ponytail, and two ragged scars crisscrossed his face. His dark cloak was caked in dried mud.

His red, wild eyes surveyed the plateau that stretched below his cave. In the distance he saw the large lake that was surrounded by three mountain peaks. Something drew him towards it, but he did not know what it was, or why. One day he would find out.

But right now he was hungry—hungry to kill. He blew his mountain horn, and two black wolverines appeared at the forest's edge. They slunk swiftly and quietly up the hill. When they reached the top, they sat down and looked at their master. Their tails twitched with impatience, and they gnashed their fangs.

"Let's hunt," said the Snow Walker.

Gliding like specters, the three ran down the mountain towards a small forest. Soon they picked up the fresh tracks of mountain goats. The wolverines' thirst for meat and the Snow Walker's thirst for blood hurried them forward, and it wasn't long before they found the makers of the tracks. A mountain goat was grazing peacefully in a small forest opening, nibbling on shrubs that poked above the snow. Nearby, her two young ones were playing in the white powder.

Silently, mercilessly, the Snow Walker and his two beasts charged at the goats. There wasn't much of a fight. The goats had no time to react, no time to run, and barely any time to be surprised.

The Snow Walker let his pets finish their feast of the mother goat, which was more than enough to satisfy their hunger. Then he turned from the blood-drenched snow, satisfied and ready to head home.

Suddenly he stopped and looked around. Something was different. His enhanced senses—a gift from the Evil One— told him that the equilibrium of the four lands had shifted.

He knew of the prophecy and the coming of the one who would gather the relics. Now he knew that the time had come to prepare. The thought intrigued him. He looked south. From where he was standing he was able to see the large, green valley, and he sensed that the Last Descendant would approach from that direction.

Now he had two tasks to complete. First: find the hiding spot of the remaining Mountain People and steal the Golden Sword. Second: capture the Last Descendant and kill him.

He looked down at his beasts, who were waiting for their next order. Goat blood dripped from their teeth.

"The one who will try to save the four lands has come of age," he growled. "We have to get ready for a special hunt."

With that, the Warlord of the North picked up the two dead kid goats, turned around and climbed back up the mountain to his cave.

CHAPTER THREE

The Watcher

Help will come in all shapes and forms. What looks ugly might be beautiful. What looks lovely might be deadly. You are the judge, but don't be prejudiced. Listen and trust.

From The Book of Erebus

Still deep in thought, Chantel selected her brown leather pants, beige blouse, green vest and brown leather boots. As she pulled the blouse over her head, her hair flopped into her face. She began to straighten it and, to her surprise, felt something different.

She glanced into the mirror. There, hanging amidst her brown curls, was a shiny golden braid. Chantel stared at it incredulously. She tugged it and it pulled at her scalp.

"Ouch!" She looked at it again in the mirror. "How can this be?"

After slipping on the rest of her clothes, she hurried down

the tower stairs and into the kitchen.

"Where did this come from?" she cried, pointing to the braid. Her voice sounded louder and angrier than she had meant it to.

Owl, in the midst of scooping eggs onto two plates, replied calmly, "The Golden Braid. It is the mark of the Princess of Freedom, as prophesized." He handed Chantel her breakfast. "Sit down and eat. I will tell you more in a minute."

Chantel sat with a thud at the oak table and curled her knees into her chest. She nibbled at a piece of toast and touched her Golden Braid. It was very soft and slid smoothly through her fingers.

When she'd finished her toast, she turned to Owl. "Please forgive my outburst."

"Never mind, my dear Chantel. You have a lot to learn, and the things I have told you so far are not easy to comprehend. And there is more—much more." Owl closed his eyes. But before he had a chance to begin, they were interrupted by **THUMP! THUMP! THUMP!**

Chantel and Owl jumped. Someone—or something— was knocking at their door.

Chantel looked at Owl anxiously. "I thought our castle was invisible, Owl."

"Stay here," Owl commanded.

He walked into the large hallway.

The hallway's walls were built from red rocks gathered from the shoreline in the land of the West and the floor was covered with flat, yellow sandstone slabs from the desert in the land of the South. At the end of the huge hallway stood two massive wooden doors constructed from the large trees of the forest in the land of the East.

Owl walked to the doors quietly and listened. "Who's there?" he finally shouted.

"The Watcher," came a deep voice from the other side of the doors. "It is time."

"Are you friend or foe?"

"What do you think? Have you forgotten what the golden hummingbird told you?"

Owl thought for a brief moment and then remembered that friends would identify themselves with the code words "It is time."

Owl opened the heavy doors, but to his surprise there was no one there. "Hello?" He looked down the small walkway that led through the courtyard towards the castle gates. The dewy grass glistened in the morning sun. He took a few steps outside.

"Hello?" he cried again.

A deep voice behind him replied, "You should be more careful when you open the door to strangers."

Owl turned around with his claws poised to attack.

"Down here!" roared an orange mouse.

"A mouse?" Owl's feathers ruffled in shock.

"Never expect the obvious," the mouse growled. "I am the Watcher, Helper and Protector of the Princess of Freedom. My name is Mouse. Mother Nature sent me. Where is the princess?"

"Chantel's in the kitchen. Follow me," said Owl.

As they entered the kitchen, Chantel crept out from behind a chair. "Who was it, Owl?" she asked.

Mouse jumped onto a chair and then onto the table. "Good morning," he said to Chantel with a gallant bow.

"This is Mouse," said Owl.

Chantel's worry dissipated. "Good morning. Welcome to our castle. For a mouse you have a very impressive voice and a strong knock."

"Actually," Mouse said indignantly, "I am not just a mouse. I am an Allactaga Tetradactyla, from the Dipodidae family, also related to the kangaroo mouse. I was sent by the golden hummingbird to be your Watcher, Helper and Protector."

Chantel took a second, more thorough look at Mouse. His ears were long and looked like rabbit ears she'd seen in books in their library. His gray and orange fur was short, and his long tail, resting on the table, had a black band near its feathery white tip. His long, thin hind feet tapped softly on the table. Four inches tall, he stood with the air of one not to be underestimated.

Despite Mouse's stance and looks, Chantel sensed that he was not as confident as he made himself out to be. She did not know where this insight came from, but it made her shiver.

"What?" Mouse said finally.

Chantel blushed, realizing that she was staring at him intently.

"Today is Chantel's birthday and the day the Golden Braid appeared," said Owl. "I was just about to explain the journey to her."

"Please don't let me interrupt you," said Mouse.

He sat on the table near a vase of wildflowers while Owl

poured a fresh cup of hot chocolate for Mouse. The cup was big enough for Mouse to bathe in. To sip the drink he had to dip his whiskers into the cup and then lick off the drops. Owl took a sip from his own beak-shaped cup, sat at the table across from Chantel and Mouse, and began to explain Chantel's quest.

CHAPTER FOUR

Chantel's Quest

When one hears stories from faraway places and does not understand their meaning, what should one do? Listen silently and pretend to understand and look smart, or be humble and ask questions to find out the real meaning of the stories? Nothing is worse than failing to find out the true meaning of what is being said and acting on wrong, assumed knowledge.

From The Book of Erebus

"The journey you shall undertake," Owl began, "will be dangerous but rewarding. Now listen closely: you must retrieve four relics—one from each of the four lands—and return them to this castle. These four relics together will release so much light power that it will free us from the Darkness and the power of the Evil One. But if the relics aren't recovered and brought here, the Evil One will destroy everything. The forests will die, the sun will vanish and the two moons will go dark.

"The relics represent the customs, values and beliefs of the people of the four lands. The Golden Sword of the mountains of the North represents sharing. The Silver Leaf of the forest of the East represents family. The Enchanted Medallion of the desert of the South represents simplicity, and the Crystal Star of the waters of the West represents truth. The first relic you must recover is the Golden Sword.

"Each relic was once guarded by a Wise One who lived in that land. The Wise Ones used the relics to guide the people in their belief of the light power, to keep them from turning to the Darkness. The Darkness, however, grew stronger, and not even the relics were able to stop people from forgetting their values and turning to the Darkness and the Evil One. Finally there was a Great War between the Evil One and the four Wise Ones, who were helped by the spirits.

"The Evil One was defeated and banished. Some say it was put into a sleep as deep as death. The Wise Ones and the leaders of the lands, believing they were free of the Evil One for good, brought their relics to this castle for safekeeping. On special occasions they would retrieve their relics to show their people and return the relics to the castle afterwards. For many moons, all was peaceful. Then, twenty moon crossings ago, a boy in the land of the North released the dark power. People worried that this might awake the Evil One. No one knew for certain if it had, until eight moon crossings ago, when a red lightning bolt from across the ocean destroyed a small village on the West Coast. It was the village of the Winged Ones. Only the Evil One can wield the red lightning bolt without the aid of a magical weapon or relic."

Owl became quiet and his eyes filled with tears. He walked over to the window that faced the courtyard of the castle, his back to Chantel and Mouse.

"Nobody in the village survived," Owl said, covering his eyes with his right wing. He paused for a while to regain his composure. "At the same time, the Wise One of the West disappeared."

Chantel shivered, sensing Owl was hiding something, just like Mouse. "Where are these feelings coming from?" she wondered.

For a long time, Owl did not speak. Suddenly he turned around and continued with new energy and an urgency in his voice. "After that, the remaining three Wise Ones came to this castle and retrieved the relics. This was part of the prophecy, something they had to do if the Evil One ever awoke. I do not know where they put the relics. They also took the fourth relic, the Crystal Star of the West.

"Like everything in our world, the relics have a good side and an evil side. The Ancient Council installed the light power into the relics to be used for protection, but the Evil One installed the dark power into them, and the dark power kills. You, as the Princess of Freedom, will eventually be able to call upon both powers, the light and the dark. No other creature can do that. But you have to learn how to use the powers wisely. Use the light power too much and it will kill you. Use the dark power too much and you will get lost and join the Evil One and kill us.

"You have other powers, too," Owl continued. "Your inner voice—your instincts and your senses—will warn you of danger and show you who your friends are. The three Wise Ones will teach you more about your talents. They will know where the relics are kept."

"So that's what I've been feeling," Chantel thought. "My inner voice has been warning me about Mouse and Owl. But why?"

"Does the Evil One know about Chantel's journey?" asked Mouse.

"We do not know where the Evil One is," replied Owl, shifting his gaze away, which made Chantel uncomfortable again, "or even who or what it is. It has been a long time since the birth of the relics. Something terrible must have happened, because at one time the Evil One was part of the spirit world that protected the lands. The Evil One's four warlords and their misguided helpers have been looking for these relics for many moon crossings. They are brutal, fearless and ruthless. They kill and destroy on a whim.

"There is a fear that soon the Evil One will return to our lands and use its lightning bolts to destroy everyone in every village. We do not have much time. The Warlord of the North knows that someone has arrived to gather the relics. He will be hunting you, Chantel, but he does not know you are the one. We can't let him or the Evil One find out who you are.

"Before you start the quest to find the Golden Sword, you must return to the place where I found you twelve moon crossings ago, and find Mother Nature. She will help you."

"When?"

"The sooner the better," Owl said. "Time is pressing. We

only have one moon crossing left. If the four relics are not in the castle by then, the light magic will be lost forever. If that happens, nothing will be able to stop the Evil One. Do you have any more questions? Do you know what you have to do?"

Chantel gulped, nodded and then stood up. "I'd better get ready," she said as she left the table and walked quickly up the tower stairs to her room.

⌒⌇⌇⌇

With trembling fingers, Chantel put on a green cloak and secured a blue pouch on her belt. She opened the weathered chest that stood in one of the corners of her room.

From the chest she took a small silver sword. Owl had made it for her three moon crossings ago. The sword's hilt fit her hand perfectly, and the sharp blade shone with a light like silvery blue moonbeams. She moved it swiftly through the air. She had practiced using it many times without Owl's knowledge.

"Should I take it?" Chantel wondered aloud.

"I would," Mouse replied.

Chantel jumped.

"Sorry," Mouse said as he hopped on top of her desk. "I just followed you to make sure you were okay."

His large eyes surveyed each of the room's windows. "You have an excellent view from up here. The mountains seem so close, the forest so green, the desert so bright and the ocean so blue. It must be hard to say good-bye."

"Yes," said Chantel, sighing.

"Have you said good-bye to your parents?"

"I have no parents. I don't know whether they are alive or not. Owl and this castle are all I have ever known. I have never seen the outside world."

"The outside world is beautiful," said Mouse, "as well as cruel and ruthless. Owl is right. Wild beasts roam the lands. But the world is not yet completely lost to the Darkness. There are still majestic mountains decorated with waterfalls and still bubbling creeks that run through large forests, and the ocean still moves freely along the rugged shoreline."

"It sounds big," Chantel said quietly. "It doesn't make sense. How can I be the Princess of Freedom when I don't know anything about the lands or being free?"

Mouse pressed his paw to his chest in a gesture of understanding. "You won't be alone," he said. "I will be with you. I will protect you and help you fulfill your quest. You might even learn things about yourself that you aren't aware of. Perhaps you'll find out what happened to your parents . . . perhaps I'll find out what happened to me . . ."

"What do you mean?" Chantel asked.

"The future lies ahead of us, and we will never find out what could have been if we keep standing here. Come on, let's go," Mouse said, ignoring Chantel's question.

Chantel put the sword into its leather sheath and secured it to her belt. Before shutting the door, she gave her room a final glance. "Good-bye," she whispered.

Owl stood in the kitchen, holding two backpacks. One was big, for Chantel, and one was small, for Mouse.

"Only two?"

"I must stay behind to guard the castle. I will be here when you return. Remember that the castle is your home, your stronghold. The Evil One and its helpers do not know who you are yet. Do not expose yourself. Be vigilant and remember: 'It is time.' Friends will identify themselves with that phrase. Above all, stay true to yourself, my lovely princess."

"You have to come," said Chantel. "You're my guardian!"

Owl shook his head.

"If you aren't coming, I won't go," Chantel protested.

Owl kept shaking his head. "I must stay with the castle. That is my duty."

Mouse jumped in. "The future is out there, not here, Chantel. You won't be alone," he said, his paw on his chest again. "I will be with you."

Chantel hesitated for a moment and then grabbed her backpack.

⁘

The huge stone wall that surrounded the castle had four open arches. They faced north, east, south and west, and each were guarded by metal gates, forged out of the black iron sand from the mountain streams and embellished with flowers and leaves.

Owl, Chantel and Mouse walked along the path to the gate that faced the land of the North. Looking closely, Chantel could see decorations she hadn't noticed before. Incorporated into the lattice, in each corner of the gate, were a finely wrought metal sword, medallion, leaf and star.

Owl took a giant bronze key from under his wing and unlocked the gates. They swung outwards without a creak.

He turned to Chantel and gave her a big hug, his wingtips tickling her ears. "Be careful. I will be waiting for you." Then he turned to Mouse and extended a claw that Mouse timidly shook with both paws. "Look after her," Owl said. "She is very precious to all of us."

"I will," replied Mouse.

"I will keep you in my heart, dear Owl," said Chantel. "And I will see you again soon."

"I certainly hope so," Owl said to himself, crossing his wings across his chest to hide his emotions.

CHAPTER FIVE

The Evil One Awakes

The past will repeat itself. Why don't people learn from their mistakes? When the time is right and emotions run high, one will turn to his dark side and break the Evil One's slumber. It takes only one person to change the world forever.

From The Book of Erebus

Summertime in the mountains was filled with many festivals and town gatherings. People from all the lands came to the mountains to celebrate feasting festivals, singing festivals and dancing festivals. There was one special festival, the Championship of the Golden Sword that only the Mountain People could attend. All the Mountain People looked forward to this festival, which revolved around a great climbing competition that the girls and boys took part in.

Twenty moon crossings ago, a young boy named Aquila Bellum was the favorite to win the championship. Although only seventeen, he was as strong and tall as a man. His hair was long and black, his skin was the color of golden sand, and his blue eyes always sparkled with energy. Called the Snow Walker because he could walk on all kinds of snow, he was the best hunter in the mountains.

Aquila Bellum trained for the competition for many moon crossings. He practiced climbing every day. He ran for miles around the mountain plateaus. He even spent hours swimming in the freezing waters of the mountain lakes. His parents always encouraged him, even though they were concerned about his strong will. Someone else was also concerned about Aquila's obsession to win: Mother Nature.

During one of Aquila's early morning runs, just as the fog started to rise out of the valley below, he saw her. She winked at him and then disappeared. Another time, as he stood shivering at the shore after a long swim in one of the many mountain lakes, she appeared and handed him a warm blanket made out of moss.

"You are very strong, Aquila Bellum. You will make your parents proud," she said. "I am watching you."

﹏﹏

On the day of the competition, Aquila Bellum was fully prepared. He towered over all the other boys and girls who had come to climb the steep cliff.

"Let's go," he yelled. "I will show you how it's done."

He grabbed one of the climbing ropes and marched towards the cliff. With a single mighty flip of the rope, he looped it around a rock at the top. Leaping from ledge to ledge, he danced up the side of the mountain with the ease of the fabled Rock Climbers that scaled the cliffs of the Endless Gorge.

Before the next boy was halfway up, Aquila Bellum hooted triumphantly from the top. The crowd below went wild. No one had ever reached the top so quickly. Aquila Bellum's parents proudly accepted all the handshakes as Aquila climbed down the cliff. He walked with open arms towards his parents.

"Well done, my son," Artos Bellum said. They hugged each other and walked to the stone table where the council of elders sat. "You deserve your victory," Artos added. "You've worked very hard. I'm proud of you."

"Thank you, father," said Aquila.

But his father's praise wasn't enough this time.

Aquila Bellum stood in front of the council of elders. Aurora, the chair of the council, rose from her seat. Her gray hair was braided into three ponytails held together with a golden bracelet. She wore the simple traditional clothing of the Mountain People: a long leather skirt, white blouse and gray felt vest. Her face was lined with age but still beautiful and strong. Her blue eyes reflected the wisdom of many years. She was almost a head shorter than Aquila, but the way she stood made her seem taller. With a single nod, she silenced the crowd. She came forward and hung a golden medallion around Aquila's neck. "Congratulations, young Aquila Bellum. You are the champion of this year's competition. Great things will come from you."

Although Aquila was filled with pride, secretly he was waiting for an even bigger prize that would be handed out that evening. "This is my year," he thought. "I will hold the most valuable item of our people in my hands, and everyone will bow and honor me."

As the sun disappeared for the day and its last rays painted the mountain peaks in spectacular colors, the Mountain People gathered on a meadow below a small plateau and waited for the arrival of the Golden Sword.

"Welcome, my people, to the night of the relic," said Aurora from the top of the plateau, dressed in a gown of shimmering rainbow colors. "We have gathered here to celebrate our ancestors and to cherish our beliefs and values. The Golden Sword will arrive soon, and we must prepare to receive it. I call upon Aquila Bellum, this year's champion, to come forward and join me."

The people looked around to find Aquila Bellum. He walked through the crowd slowly, enjoying every second of his procession. Finally he reached the front and joined Aurora on the plateau. The crowd burst into applause. People started to chant Aquila's name.

"Silence." Aurora's voice stilled even the birds. "It's time to welcome our Wise One, Eronimus Finsh. He has brought the Golden Sword from the hidden castle for our annual festivities."

In a burst of blue light, Eronimus Finsh appeared beside Aurora, holding the Sword. It shimmered brightly in the sun's fading red glow.

"'For Us to Share,'" cried Aurora, as Eronimus handed the Sword to Aquila.

Aquila shook as he grasped its hilt. Warmth spread through his hands and body. Slowly, he lifted the sword over his head. The crowd bowed in respect. Even Aurora and Eronimus knelt on the plateau.

Aquila saw the admiration in the eyes of the people below. He had never felt so powerful, so strong. He didn't want the feeling to end.

His heart turned cold. The Golden Sword started to shine bright red, redder than the sun's rays. A tremor rocked the ground. People lifted their heads and jumped to their feet, moving away from the plateau.

"What's happening?" they cried, staring from the red Sword to Aquila's eyes, which were no longer blue but speckled with red. Aquila saw the fear in their faces and heard their muffled cries. "How small and insignificant they look," he thought. "I am the one who is strong and in control. I am the one who will lead them. I am the one with the power." His eyes turned completely red. He shook with excitement and lust for power. He knew his time had come. He was a man now, a man who would rule and conquer the lands.

Eronimus Finsh reached for the Sword, but Aquila refused to let it go and pushed him away with his elbow.

As Aquila tightened his grip on the hilt, another tremor rocked the land.

On a tiny island surrounded by red mist, in a cave of total blackness, the Evil One opened her eyes and rattled her chains.

She smiled.

"It always starts with one," she whispered to herself, "the one who is strong and who is tempted by the power I instilled in the Golden Sword during its creation." The Evil One could feel the one who was now holding the Golden Sword. "Thank you for awakening me. Now you must help me take my revenge. Now you must help set me free."

⁓〰⁓

"I have earned this," Aquila Bellum yelled, his eyes fixed on the Golden Sword. "This is my time—my time to rule."

"It is not your time, my son," his father cried, pushing through the crowd. "It is not your time!"

"So you don't believe in me, father? You never believed in me." Aquila's voice was full of anger and hatred.

"I believe in you. I love you. You are my son." His father reached the plateau. "But this is wrong. Don't you feel it? The Darkness is starting to overwhelm you. Do not follow it! It will lead to disaster."

Aquila Bellum turned his head. The red glow around the Sword turned an even more brilliant bloody color.

CRACK! A red lightning bolt burst from the tip of the Golden Sword. It traveled up high before it turned west, towards the island where the Evil One had been banished to thirty-five moon crossings ago.

⁓〰⁓

SNAP! One of the three enchanted glass chains that held the Evil One broke.

"Two more, and then I will be free!" cried the Evil One in delight.

The earth shook again. Heavy red waves raced towards the land of the West, signaling what was to come.

⁓✳⁓

Aquila Bellum's hands burned. He dropped the red-hot Sword and fell to his knees. The person who wielded the Golden Sword controlled the red lightning bolt of the Darkness, the most powerful force of the four lands. More than anything, Aquila wanted to wield that force. Despite the pulsing pain in his hands, he reached for the Sword, but he was too late.

Eronimus Finsh had picked up the Golden Sword and vanished with it as suddenly as he had appeared. The Wise One knew he must return the relic to its protective place, to the hidden castle in the center of the four lands.

"Come back!" Aquila screamed. "The Sword is mine!" He jumped up and clawed at the air. Spit ran down the sides of his mouth. He looked like a beast. His father tried to calm him, but Aquila pushed him aside.

"Be careful, father," Aquila hissed. Then he turned around and jumped off the plateau. His father, mother and sister and all the Mountain People watched in horror as Aquila ran away and was swallowed by the darkness of the night.

CHAPTER SIX

Chantel's Journey Begins

Chantel and Mouse walked through the gates, which swung closed quietly behind them as fog shrouded the castle. The sun had reached its midday position. The air was warm and sweet.

"Finally," Chantel thought. She had always wanted to know how the air smelled outside the castle walls. She'd always wanted to walk through the trees she saw from her castle windows. She looked around. The leaves were all shades of green. Some were even tinged with yellow and orange. The air smelled like honey, grass and wet mud. The thick grass that grew along the path was dotted with colorful flowers of all shapes and sizes.

There were so many sounds, too. Bees were humming, birds twittered at each other, and breezes whispered through the leaves. Every so often, a howl quieted the bees and birds and even the breezes. The howls made Chantel's back tingle and her arms twitch. They made her want to turn around and run back into Owl's big, soft wings. But she forced her feet to step forward, away from the castle.

Mouse walked slightly ahead. Although he sensed Chantel's unease, he was too busy to comfort her. His ears and eyes moved constantly in all directions, looking for unusual movements and listening for displaced sounds.

As they traveled farther away from the gates of the castle, Chantel's steps grew more confident. There was no turning back. Although the howls were frightening, her surroundings were beautiful and did not seem dangerous. When they reached the bottom of the hill, Chantel turned around to have one last look at the castle, but it was gone. All she could see was a small hill with a cloud hovering over it and the vast blue sky.

"I'd better remember this place so I can find my way home," Chantel said, noting a particularly twisted oak tree with a big nest perched in its top branches. "If we get separated, we will meet here. Okay, Mouse?"

"Agreed, but we will not get separated," he answered, his eyes peering elsewhere.

"What are you looking for?"

"Enemies," he said.

"Like what?"

"We will encounter them soon enough if we are not careful. Some are terribly ugly. There are merciless hyenas with big, crooked mouths and long, sharp teeth. There are brutal wolverines with big paws and long claws. On the other hand, some enemies are quite beautiful, like the purple songbird of the West. Its song is so beautiful and seductive that if you listen to it you will get lost, and then the bird will trap you and peck you to death with its beak. But for now, we do not have to worry. They seldom come this close to the center of the four lands."

Mouse, however, continued to be vigilant. He did not want to scare Chantel too much on the first day of her quest, but he knew that their enemies were growing in numbers every day, and it was likely they would spread to the center of the four realms.

Mouse and Chantel did not travel in a straight line towards their first destination, the place where Owl had found Chantel so many moon crossings ago. Mouse used the most secluded paths he could find. He did not want to expose them more than was necessary. Chantel didn't notice. She followed Mouse and tried to enjoy herself, looking around and smelling the odd flower, and even spying what looked like a fox den. Her thoughts turned to her friend Fawn.

One day Fawn had appeared in the castle's courtyard. He must have crawled through the gates. It had taken Chantel days of patient coaxing, holding out bits of meat, before the fox would come close to her. Before long, however, Fawn had become her best friend—her only friend other than Owl. Fawn even shared her seat in the kitchen and slept beside her bed.

"Will Mouse become my friend, too?" wondered Chantel as she hiked along. She thought about the effort it had taken to charm shy Fawn into becoming her friend. Mouse was clearly different. It was she who felt shy around him, perhaps because he showed such confidence in the outside world.

When they came to a bubbling creek, they followed it into

the forest that led up to the mountains. By that time, the sun was falling and the shadowed spots were increasing. Mouse looked around and stopped in front of a giant oak tree with strong branches.

"It's late," he said. "The sun is getting ready to rest and will soon vanish behind the mountains in the West. Climb up here, Chantel, and find a nice branch to sleep on."

"Sleep in a tree?" Chantel squealed. She blushed at the tone of her own voice.

"Yes, it's safer to sleep in a tree than on the ground," replied Mouse. "The ground might be softer, but if you use your backpack and your cloak you can make yourself a decent bed on one of the thick branches."

After a few failed attempts, Chantel managed to hoist herself onto the lowest branches, scratching her elbow in the process. She settled on the first thick branch she reached. Mouse selected a higher branch, where he had a good view of the surrounding forest. The lake in the distance shimmered—half icy-silvery blue, half fiery-dark red—in the shifting light of the two moons.

"It's a two-day journey through the forest to the lake," he told Chantel. "From there we will be able to see the waterfall. Are you comfortable?"

"I'm okay."

"Have a good rest, Chantel."

"You too, Mouse."

But Chantel didn't close her eyes. The branch wasn't comfortable at all, and she was afraid of falling off. The night song of the crickets and the bellowing cries of the forest frogs were a big contrast to the silence of her tower room. Her mind was filled with other noises, too: worries and wonderings, and questions about what had happened in the past and what would happen in the future.

"Mouse?" she whispered.

"Yes."

"How do you know this area so well?"

"I have been around for many years. I look younger than I really am." He smiled. "I have traveled all four lands many times. Different people with different cultures and values live in each place, but they all share one thing in common: they love their land. Many moon crossings ago, the people of the different lands used to meet and exchange their knowledge, recipes, ideas and stories. The Mountain People traveled to the West to meet with the Winged Ones, the Forest People traveled to the South to enjoy festivals with the Desert Tribes, and so on."

"Why did the Evil One awake?" Chantel asked. "What did Owl mean about the boy releasing the Darkness?"

"Are you sure you want to know? It isn't a pleasant story."

"I'm not afraid!"

"I didn't mean . . ." Mouse sighed, and then began, "This is what I've been told: During one of the festive events of the Mountain People, twenty moon crossings ago, something terrible happened. A young boy touched the Golden Sword, and the dark magic hidden in it was released. Usually, any human touched by the dark magic dies, but somehow this mountain boy survived, and he ran away. It's rumored that he lives in the mountains like a monster. A couple of moon crossings ago, some Mountain People were found dead. Their bodies had been ripped to pieces, and human bite marks were found on a few of their bones." Mouse shook. "After that boy touched the Sword and awoke the Evil One, the Darkness began to spread relentlessly and the unity of our diverse lands fell apart. Now the lands are filled with traps and ugly, dangerous creatures. Most of those who have stayed true to themselves are in hiding. They are afraid and do not know how to help themselves. You will unite them. I'm proud to be with you."

Mouse peered through the leaves and gave Chantel a warm smile. "Now you must go to sleep. We need to rest for our long journey tomorrow. Good night, Chantel, Princess of Freedom."

"Good night, Mouse." Chantel gulped. Thinking about the boy and the Evil One was worse than worrying about falling off the branch. She tried not to think about either by counting the stars in the sky. It was a long time, however, before her eyes finally closed in sleep.

Chantel dreamt of foreign places and people, of colorful rainbows and of a young boy with red eyes, running barefoot in the snow.

Mouse slept with one eye open. It was a habit that had saved his life many times. Even while sleeping his ears constantly moved. Throughout the night, he heard a few howls, but none were loud enough, and thus near enough, to wake him.

*

Early in the morning, however, a noise did make him worry enough that he opened both eyes in alarm. A nine-legged, poisonous spider the size of a cat, with red stripes across its hairy body and long fangs, was crawling around the base of the tree. Mouse did not move or make a sound. He hoped that Chantel would continue to sleep and not make a sound either, because this type of spider didn't sense by smell or sight, but by sound. Mouse did not want to start the morning fighting the hairy, long-legged creature.

Chantel slept soundly and the spider left. In fact, she slept longer than Mouse had expected.

⁓✤⁓

At first, when Chantel finally woke up, she did not know where she was. Luckily she remembered before she rolled off the branch. She stretched along the branch carefully. She was stiff and her back hurt. She looked down and became dizzy and almost slipped. Her cloak slid off the branch and floated to the ground slowly like a leaf. "How am I supposed to get down?" she thought. "Getting up here was hard enough."

"Mouse!" she called out.

There was no answer. She looked around but could not see him.

"MOUSE!" she yelled louder. When she got no response again, her thoughts began to jump irrationally. Her Golden Braid hung like a weight from her head.

"Did Mouse abandon me? Is this what happened when I was a baby? Did my parents abandon me?"

Chantel began to envision her parents leaving her in the forest. Then the images in her head became even darker. She saw Owl stealing her from her parents and lying to her about her quest. Faint rustling from below the tree brought her out of her dark thoughts. She looked down and saw Mouse emerging from a thick, spiny bush.

"Where have you been?" she yelled angrily. Tears of fear and frustration ran down her cheeks. "Why did you abandon me?"

"I didn't abandon you. I went to get us some breakfast. Look." Mouse pulled a large leaf behind him like a sled. On the leaf was a pile of berries stacked in a neat pyramid. "Why are you so angry?"

"This is my first morning in the wild," Chantel continued to yell as she climbed down the tree. Now that she wasn't thinking about the height, she had no difficulty getting down. "How would you feel if you woke up alone? Imagine!" She was so angry that she felt like stomping on the berries.

"The Darkness," Mouse whispered. "It's in the air. Chantel, listen to me. You've been touched by the Darkness. Stay true to yourself. Focus."

Chantel tensed. She closed her eyes.

She remembered the weight of her Golden Braid. Her senses had been warning her. She thought about what she knew. She knew Owl had not killed her parents. She knew Mouse would not abandon her. When she opened her eyes, she was shaking violently, but her anger was gone.

"Is that how it feels when you become possessed by the Darkness?" asked Chantel. "That's awful. Those poor people and creatures that have fallen under its spell . . ."

Mouse nodded and said, "But be careful. Don't feel too sorry for them or you will underestimate them. You will have more encounters with the Darkness, so be aware. You have to fight it off. You must not allow it to overwhelm your mind. If it does, you will be lost to it. You may often have to battle between your good side and your evil side. Come, let's have something to eat. You need your strength."

Chantel ate the berries one by one. They were sweet, delicious and juicy. Her fingers were soon stained blue.

"Here, I also found some worms," Mouse said.

He untied another leaf that lay by his side. Inside, three yellow, slimy worms, each as thick as Chantel's little finger, were trying to wiggle their way to freedom. Chantel wrinkled her nose.

"Try them," Mouse said, smiling at Chantel's disgusted look. "They are rich in protein. Do not think of them as worms but as nourishment necessary for the quest. Out here you have to eat everything. You can't be choosy. You never know when you will find something to eat again."

Chantel blushed. At the castle she had never had to worry about her next meal. The castle garden, which she'd carefully tended, had provided most of her food. But out here, it was different. She hadn't even thanked Mouse for the berries, and now she was refusing the other food he'd foraged for her. She took a worm and put it in her mouth. The warm, slippery body moved across her tongue and almost found its way down her throat by itself. She grimaced and gulped.

"Your first test of bravery." Mouse laughed. "Well done."

After they had finished their breakfast, they packed their belongings and continued the journey towards the mountains.

"We still have a long way to go," Mouse said. "What do you think about the forest, Chantel?"

Chantel still felt a little queasy from the worms, but she looked around. "The leaves look green, the grass looks green, and the moss looks green and inviting. I feel the moisture in the air and smell the mushrooms on the ground, so I think the forest must be healthy. But some of the trees have lost all their leaves, even though it's summer, and some of the grass is brown. And yesterday I saw a few dead birds by the side of the path."

"Very good. You're observant, and that's important. Indeed, those are the signs of the Darkness. Nature is no longer fully healthy. It is slowly dying."

They walked quietly for a while, side by side. Chantel, now fully aware of the destruction that was going on in the forest, saw more dead trees, dead grass and dead animals. She had to distract herself from the realization of what the Darkness was doing to nature. She turned to Mouse.

"Why don't you tell me about yourself?" Chantel asked. "Where are you from, Mouse?"

CHAPTER SEVEN

Mouse's Past

Mouse took a deep breath, contemplating just how much he should tell her. He had been worrying about this moment. His past was something he'd rather forget.

"My story is not a happy one," he said finally. "I grew up in a sandy, dry area along the border between the forest and the desert, where the land of the East meets the land of the South. My twenty brothers and twelve sisters and I were always fighting for food and attention. There were just too many of us, but that is the nature of your average mouse family. Soon I found out that I was different. I could run faster, I could jump higher and I was stronger. And there was something else: if I wanted to, I could transform into a giant mouse—ten times bigger than a desert sand cat. But on my thirteenth birthday, something terrible happened.

"I was very angry. I have forgotten why I was so angry, but my anger was so great that I changed without wanting to. I couldn't control myself. I picked up huge rocks and threw them hundreds of meters away. One of the rocks hit the den of a neighboring mouse family. When I calmed down, I changed back into my normal small self. But it didn't matter. My family and all the neighbors were afraid of me from that moment on.

"I began to go on long trips to the other lands, but I always had the need to return home. Then something happened that made me leave for good. In the middle of the night, after I had just returned from the East, my family attacked me. They came with axes, knives and bats. I fought them off and ran away, but I was badly injured. I ran for a long time and lost much blood. I must have wandered around for a few days. Finally I collapsed on a patch of grass beneath a canopy of leaves.

"When I woke up, I was bandaged and lying on a bed of soft, warm moss in a cave of crystals. Then I saw the most beautiful being I have ever seen, and I started to cry because I knew I was finally safe and loved."

"Who did you see?" asked Chantel.

"Mother Nature," replied Mouse. "I saw Mother Nature floating towards me, her bare feet just skimming the ground. She was wearing a dress made from green and red leaves. Her lips were orange, like a winter sunset, and her eyes were as brown as the richest earth. 'You are safe here,' she said to me. 'Rest for a few more days and you will recover fully.'"

Mouse paused for a moment. His eyes were full of tears. He perked his ears, listening for danger, but didn't hear anything except the leaves whispering their song of sorrow and loss of health, a song Mouse recognized but Chantel had yet to learn. The birds understood it, too, and their dance in the sky was mournful, full of long loops and low, soft cries.

"After three days, I saw Mother Nature again," Mouse continued. "By then I felt much better and had almost completely recovered, just as she had said. She looked deep into my eyes and said, 'I see that you are true of heart and strong in will. I need you to help me fight the Darkness.' I wondered how I could be worthy enough to help Mother Nature? I was honored.

"She continued, 'Six moon crossings from now, on the night of the next eclipse, the Princess of Freedom will come of age. She is the one who will free us from the Darkness. Her name is Chantel, and you shall be her Watcher. Find the castle behind the mist. Guide and protect her on her quests. She is our only hope.'

"I spent the last six moon crossings traveling the lands, seeing the changes and the evil the Darkness has wrought. Every day I thought about you and Mother Nature's message. Then, finally, the eclipse neared. I searched for several days to find your castle. If Mother Nature had not aided me, I would have never found it. And now here we are, together at the start of your first quest."

Mouse stopped again. He listened. Nothing. All was calm and peaceful.

"Thank you for sharing your story with me," said Chantel. "Could you show me your gift?"

"What do you mean?"

"Your transformation."

"No," he said. He quickened his pace to put some distance between them.

"So there is still more to Mouse's story," thought Chantel. "I wonder what he's hiding."

Near the end of the day, Mouse selected another big tree to sleep in. Chantel did not look forward to another night on a hard branch, but she didn't complain. She trusted Mouse's choice of sleeping spots, and once again, after staring at the stars and the two moons through the layered leaves above her, she finally fell asleep.

That's when the nightmares began. Instead of rainbows, she faced dark, faceless creatures with red eyes and long claws that chased her through thickets of dead flowers and leafless bushes. The branches cut into her skin and tore at her hair. Just as the deadly creatures were about to grab her, she woke up, drenched in sweat. It was early morning, and the sun's first rays glimmered in the East.

Exhausted, she climbed down the tree and ate her breakfast, even the worms, without saying a word. Never before had she had such dark and frightening dreams. "Where are they coming from?" she wondered. "What do they mean?"

CHAPTER EIGHT

Mother Nature

For as long as I can remember, Mother Nature has been here. Even before my time, she traveled the plains, mountains, forests and grasslands. She suffers with each dying tree, each poisoned river and each animal's death. Even though she was strong enough to fight the Evil One in the past, the strain is leaving its mark. She becomes weaker every day.

From The Book of Erebus

By midmorning, Chantel and Mouse reached the lake and waterfall. Green willows stood along the shore. Their branches hung low and dangled in the crystal blue water. Mist from the waterfall cloaked the trees and cooled Chantel's hot cheeks.

Tiny star-shaped flowers dotted the moss-covered ground. Each flower had seven petals, and each petal was a different color so that the flowers looked like little rainbows. Chantel sat down, careful not to sit on any of the flowers. The ground was springy and soft.

"I have to leave you now, Chantel," Mouse said. "This is the place where you will meet Mother Nature. Be ready and be prepared."

Mouse's voice sounded muffled, as if it were coming through a thick fog.

"Why? Don't abandon me," Chantel pleaded.

"What Mother Nature has to tell you is for your ears only. I will see you . . ."

Chantel didn't hear Mouse's last words. Her eyelids had become so heavy that she could no longer hold them up.

A few minutes after Mouse left, a golden hummingbird appeared out of the mist. It hovered over Chantel's sleeping body for a few moments to make sure they were alone. Then the bird landed beside Chantel. First its beak and then its wings and claws began to shiver and change.

Within moments, in place of the hummingbird stood a beautiful woman. Her hair was shiny green and covered with diamonds and crystals. Two amethysts hung from her pointy ears, and she was cloaked in a dress of interwoven leaves, just as Mouse had described. Her weathered skin glowed. She knelt down beside Chantel and brushed her hand across the girl's face. A warm breeze gently roused Chantel from her enchanted slumber.

The sun was behind the woman. Chantel could only see her outline, but she knew at once it was Mother Nature.

"Good morning, Chantel. Did you have a good rest on my soft moss?" Mother Nature's voice was little louder than a hum. Her breath smelled like mint.

"Am I dreaming?" Chantel asked.

"You must decide that for yourself, Chantel."

Chantel pinched her arm and nothing changed. "I must be awake."

"Good. You have to be wide awake and attentive, because what I have to tell you is very important, and there is not much time. The friends of the Evil One seem to be everywhere these days." Mother Nature took a deep breath. It sounded like the wind. "You are our last hope. Mouse told you the story about the boy of the North, the one who had touched the Golden Sword. Indeed, he did wake the Evil One. And the Evil One did something to him, too.

"The boy, Aquila Bellum, was not evil, just ambitious and proud, but now he hates his people. The dark power he felt in the Golden Sword made him turn to his dark side. He swore an allegiance to the Evil One. As a reward, the Evil One gave him the power of telepathy, strength and near immortality. The boy has grown into a man now—a wicked, heartless warlord. He appears out of nowhere, kills and then vanishes. To prove his worthiness to the Evil One he committed a very terrible crime, so terrible that I cannot speak of it."

Mother Nature paused; her brow furrowed. She was in constant pain because of what was happening to her. "Over many moon crossings, he has been contacting other creatures and convincing them to trust their dark sides. Those who refused, he has simply killed. The more the misguided ones grow in number, the more I wither, while the Evil One gains strength. Eventually the Evil One will be strong enough to break all its chains and return to the four lands. Unless you find the four relics, we are all doomed."

"But why me?"

"You were born during a very unusual and special eclipse of the moons."

"Like the eclipse I saw on my birthday?" asked Chantel.

"Yes, except that on the night you were born the silvery-blue moon moved in front of the red moon, which is even rarer than the red coming in front of the blue. Any eclipse, however, is a special event. Good and evil are opposites, but a harmony lies between them, and the moons' alignment represents this. You alone can access this harmony, a harmony that is more powerful than either extreme. You have to find the four Wise Ones, they will . . ." Mother Nature suddenly became quiet. She raised her head and listened. Suddenly she transformed back into a golden hummingbird.

"I must leave you now, Chantel," the hummingbird said. "We have been discovered. Hide behind that big rock. Tomorrow, look into the rainbow in the waterfall and you will find the Magic Staff. The Magic Staff is a powerful tool that will be of invaluable service on your quest. With it and Mouse, you will be well protected. Then go into the mountains, to the big plateau overlooking the valley. There you will find Eronimus Finsh, the Wise One of the North. He will teach you how to use the Staff and help you find the Golden Sword."

With those final words, Mother Nature flew into the mist.

"Wait!" cried Chantel. "I have more questions. Please don't go!" But the hummingbird had already disappeared.

The warm wind that had woken her so gently had changed into a cold breeze. Chantel started to shiver. She heard the roaring of the waterfall in the distance.

Her Golden Braid felt very heavy and she remembered Mother Nature's words.

Chantel ducked behind the rock and covered herself with her cloak. She tried to stay as still and quiet as possible. For a long time, everything was silent, except for the shrieks of birds in the distance. She breathed slowly and quietly.

Then she heard sharp claws scratching over the ground where she and Mother Nature had met and faint growling, as if from a wild bear. Something big and heavy was approaching her hiding spot. It began to howl.

Even through the cloak, Chantel could smell the foul breath of the beast. She tried to remain as motionless as the rock. She held her breath and listened to the loud snuffling. Her heart thumped wildly.

The beast stood on the other side of Chantel's hiding spot and sniffed. For a long time it stood there like that, its huge, black nostrils sucking the air in and out. Finally it turned around and began to howl again. Chantel listened intently. Goose bumps covered her body, and her braid was heavy—so heavy that it hurt her temples.

Then the snuffling and scratching became fainter. The beast was moving away. At last the threatening sounds disappeared altogether. Still Chantel dared not move. Her legs began to cramp. Where was Mouse? After a long while Chantel mustered the courage to take a peek. The sun was gone, and Chantel couldn't see a thing. As one of the two moons slid from behind the clouds, the area around the rock lit up in a mysterious silvery light. A circle of lilies lay around her and on top of the rock.

"For your protection," she heard Mother Nature's voice in her mind.

Chantel looked around. Everything was quiet. Even the waterfall seemed hushed.

There was a sudden noise. Someone or something pulled at her cloak. Chantel spun around, drawing out her sword.

"Stop! It's me. It's Mouse."

She gasped with relief. "You scared me! Did you see the monster?"

"Monster? What monster?"

"The one that left these large tracks. Look." She pointed to the ground in front of the rock, realizing just how close the monster had come to her hiding spot. A few more inches and it would have been right on top of her.

"Why didn't it find me?" Chantel wondered, but then she remembered the circle of lilies.

"It looks like the tracks of a Phacochoerus, a warthog," Mouse said. "But this one has hooves with claws and must weigh at least four hundred pounds. I wonder what it's doing up here. They usually stay in their home in the South, where it's warm."

"I don't know," Chantel said. "But I know that Mother Nature was afraid of it, and if she's afraid, I'm afraid, too!"

"Come. We should hurry," replied Mouse. "It might return. I found a good sleeping spot."

"Another tree?"

"Yes," Mouse admitted, "another tree."

As she followed Mouse away from the water's edge,

Chantel was filled with unease. Where had Mouse been while the warthog prowled so close to her? Why wouldn't he transform for her? Wasn't Mouse supposed to be her Protector?

CHAPTER NINE

The Magic Staff

Nestled in a comfortable branch high up in the crown of the tree, Chantel bunched up her cloak for a pillow. The night air was not too cold. She was getting better in preparing her bed on a branch. It was peaceful, almost magical, to be so close to the two moons and the bright stars.

"Tell me more about the Evil One, Mouse."

"No one knows who the Evil One is. If someone does know, he or she is keeping it secret. But the Evil One knows about the prophecy. The Evil One knows about the Golden Braid. You must be careful to keep your hair covered."

"So why don't I just cut my braid off?" Chantel asked.

Mouse shook his head firmly. "First, how will your friends know who you are? Second, I don't think you can. It's not like regular hair. It's magical and permanent, like a birthmark. So for now, don't use your cloak as a pillow. Instead, hide your hair under its hood."

As Chantel unrolled her cloak and put it back on, Mouse added, hesitantly, "How . . . how was Mother Nature?"

Chantel sighed. "Beautiful, just like you'd said. Tomorrow we will retrieve the Magic Staff from the waterfall."

"Did . . . did she say anything about me?"

"No. There wasn't much time."

"Oh," said Mouse, disappointed. "Good night, Chantel."

"Good night, Mouse."

<hr />

A tingling sensation woke Chantel early in the morning. It was still dark. The red and the blue moons had traveled far across the sky, and the sun was still asleep. The red moon glowed brighter than the blue. Chantel looked at it and a cold shiver ran down her back.

"Keep still," Mouse whispered. "We have unwanted company."

Flapping sounds surrounded the tree, like the beating of hundreds of wings. The air was filled with movement. Chantel turned around slowly and stared into two beady, yellow eyes.

"Who are you?" a high-pitched voice demanded.

"I am a wanderer looking for precious stones," Chantel replied, surprised at her own quick lie.

"Do not get off your track, wanderer, or you will find yourself in places you do not want to be in."

"I will be careful," Chantel said in a respectful manner.

"You'd better! My name is Brutus, and I am the leader of the Night Fliers."

He hissed at Chantel with his long, sticky tongue and opened his mouth to show off his sharp fangs. Then he turned and, joined by many other leathery creatures, flew away into the darkness. The night became quiet again.

"What were they?" whispered Chantel.

"Desmodus Rotundus—Vampire Bats," muttered Mouse. "They are ugly creatures—quite harmless when they are alone, but deadly in a group. They are informants to the Warlord. From dusk to dawn they patrol the region of the North, just below the mountains, searching for warm-blooded victims to feed on. I guess you are not their blood type."

"Very funny, Mouse," Chantel said. "Do you think they saw through my lie?"

"No," Mouse replied. "Otherwise you would no longer be sitting on your branch. For now they are gone and we are safe, but I'll bet we will see them again."

⟶⟅⟆⟵

After the encounter with the Night Fliers, neither Chantel nor Mouse could get back to sleep, so they got up as soon as the sun's first rays turned the sky in the East a light pink. White mist covered the valley. For several hours they journeyed along narrow, winding paths before they reached the place where the water from a river above fell over the mountain cliff and into a deep, round pool. The water pounded down so hard that it whipped up white foam that floated to the sides of the pool. Cool mist rose up from the water like steam.

Chantel and Mouse sat down and waited patiently while the sun climbed in the sky. Finally the sun was high enough so that her rays created a rainbow in the waterfall's mist.

At first the colors of the rainbow were weak, but as the sun climbed higher, the colors grew stronger until they were so bright that they looked solid and tangible, as if they had been painted on canvas. The red was as deep and soft as Fawn's fur had been, and the indigo reminded Chantel of the color of Owl's favorite flower that grew in the shade of the castle.

"Where is the Magic Staff?" Mouse asked.

"I don't know. Mother Nature said to look into the rainbow."

They both stared very hard at the rainbow, but all they could see were the colors.

"'Look into' can also mean explore or examine," said Mouse. "I wonder if you should try touching the rainbow. Maybe the Staff is inside."

"That's silly," said Chantel.

"Maybe, but who would try to touch a rainbow, especially if it's in a waterfall?" replied Mouse.

Chantel walked as close to the splashing water as possible and reached out to touch the rainbow. As the colors surrounded first her hand and then her arm, Chantel felt something solid. She grabbed it. It was round and wooden, but it would not budge. "The Magic Staff!" she thought. "Mouse was right!"

She pulled harder, but a hand clutched her arm and pulled her into the waterfall.

"Help!" she screamed, water filling her mouth.

Mouse froze. His body trembled and his skin began to stretch, but his mind wouldn't let him change. He remembered the time when he had changed into the Mighty Warrior to help his little brother. He had succeeded, but at the same time he had broken his brother's arms and legs. Mouse had no control over the Mighty Warrior. Mouse was afraid that the Mighty Warrior might kill Chantel, so he just stood there, unable to move, unable to help the one he was supposed to protect.

Inside the waterfall, Chantel struggled against an invisible force. She kicked and screamed, but did not hit anything solid. Water poured over her head and shoulders, completely drenching her body, but she held fast to the Staff. Suddenly two blue eyes a shade darker than the water appeared in front of her.

"Who dares to touch the Magic Staff?"

"My name is Chantel. I am the Princess of Freedom," she cried, swallowing mouthfuls of water. "I need the Staff."

"You may need it, but do you deserve it?" The blue eyes blinked. The Staff jerked in Chantel's hands. She held on to it with all her strength, weakening as she swallowed more water.

"No one has ever retrieved the Magic Staff. They all gave up because they did not believe. They did not want to die. So what will you do, princess? Will you give up, too?"

"I will not give up. I am not weak," she gasped. Chantel put her head down to protect the opening of her mouth against the endless rush of water and gulped for air. "I am the one who will free those who are true at heart."

"That sounds powerful, but do you believe it?"

"I will not give it up!" she sputtered.

"You will not give it up even though you will drown? Even though you will die? I am the protector of the Staff. Do you think I will give it up?"

The words echoed in Chantel's head.

"I don't care. I will get the Staff!" she whispered with her last breath.

Chantel's mind started to spin. Her heart was pounding and her lungs hurt, but she did not let go of the Staff. She tightened her grip. She fought for air, but the more she fought, the more water entered her mouth and her lungs. Slowly the pounding in her ears increased until her body went numb and darkness surrounded her.

"You will not give it up? Well, then, farewell," were the last words she heard.

⁓⁂⁓

Mouse stood beside her as she opened her eyes. She was lying in the grass near the waterfall, coughing wildly. When her lungs cleared, she sat up slowly. The rainbow was gone, and she held the Magic Staff. It was a dark brown stick, two feet long, with a pulsating crystal mounted at its top end. The crystal was clear, like a diamond, and all seven colors of the rainbow swirled and shone inside it.

"Well done," Chantel heard Mother Nature's voice say in her head. "No one but the Princess of Freedom could have taken the Magic Staff from the rainbow."

Chantel's lungs still burned, but she smiled at Mother Nature's praise. She stood up and felt strong and proud. "Where do I go from here, Mother Nature?" Chantel thought.

"Follow the path to the North. It will lead you to the Endless Gorge. On the other side of the Gorge, you will find the Wise One of the North." Mother Nature's voice began to fade. "He lives in the lower mountains."

Chantel turned to Mouse, who was hunched in a ball on the ground. He looked very small.

"Did you hear Mother Nature's words, too?" she asked.

Mouse shook his head. He could not look at Chantel; he was too ashamed.

"Are you okay?" he asked quietly.

"I'm fine. I almost drowned, but I hung on. I retrieved the Magic Staff."

"I . . . I'm sorry," muttered Mouse. "I should have . . ."

"It's okay." She smiled at Mouse to let him know that she didn't mind. She had proven the strength of her own determination, both to herself and to Mother Nature. But she was curious. Why was Mouse so upset, and why hadn't he helped her?

"We have to head to the Endless Gorge and then go to the lower mountains," she said aloud.

"How do you know?"

"Mother Nature told me."

Mouse covered his eyes with his paws and shook his head slightly. "Mother Nature doesn't trust me any more," he thought. "Otherwise I would have been able to hear her, too." His small, round eyes filled with tears. "Why couldn't I transform?"

He got up slowly and started to walk towards the Endless Gorge. He took the lead once again, even though this time he felt more like following.

CHAPTER TEN

The Rock Climber

We walk in different directions and meet different people. Although some become friends and others pass us by, in the end we are all alike. We all have hearts and souls, and we all search for the same place. But only with the help of those who love us will we find our home.

From The Book of Erebus

After walking for a few hours, they caught sight of the edge of the Endless Gorge in the distance. A thin layer of fog, rising up from the abyss, formed a transparent wall along the edge. The other side of the Gorge was far away, and there was no bridge in sight.

Chantel gulped. "How will we cross this?"

"I don't know. The Gorge is very wide and endlessly deep," Mouse replied. "If you slip and fall in, that's it. You're lost forever. Didn't Mother Nature tell you how we could cross? To go around it would take weeks."

Chantel shook her head and continued to walk forward. All of a sudden the ground beneath her feet shuddered. The earth slid away like a trap door. Mouse saw the hole opening, but he couldn't react fast enough. Before he could catch Chantel, she disappeared into the ground, dropping down into a black pit.

"What's happening? Help!" Chantel cried as she fell through clouds of dust and dirt.

"I have to separate you from Mouse," Chantel heard Mother Nature say. "Mouse is not ready yet. He is still unsure of himself and can't control his gift. He might be of more danger to you than help. The retrieval of the Magic Staff was a test for both of you. You passed it, but Mouse failed. For now it is best that you continue your journey alone. Somebody is waiting for you at the end of this tunnel. Do not be afraid."

Chantel continued to fall, but now she was silent and calm, even as the tunnel narrowed and the sides began to scrape against her skin. The clouds of dust grew thicker, and her nose and ears filled with dirt. Just as breathing started to become difficult and she began to panic again, she saw a small light below her feet that became brighter and larger very quickly. With a sudden whoosh, Chantel shot out of the tunnel and into the air. She flew like an arrow across the width of the Gorge, but she didn't make it to the other side. Just as the rocks on the side of the cliff came into sight, Chantel, screaming, began to drop down . . . down, down, down into the Endless Gorge.

⚊ᶠᶠᶠᶠᶠ⚊

Meanwhile, Mouse was too stunned to move. He had lost Chantel. Again. He had failed her. Again. At last his feet unfroze, and he ran as fast as he could, reaching the edge of the Endless Gorge just in time to see Chantel fly out of the tunnel. He heard her scream and saw her disappear into the thick mist. Her screams slowly faded away.

⚊ᶠᶠᶠᶠᶠ⚊

Chantel's fall ended as abruptly as it began.

THUMP! She landed on something hard and solid. When she opened her eyes, she saw that she was sitting on a large, gray stone. Five towers made up of individual rocks surrounded her. They were of the same color and composition as the cliff rocks. Suddenly the five towers started to move. Chantel stood up and realized that she was standing on the palm of a huge hand. The towering rocks were fingers.

"Caught you!" a rumbling voice said above her head. "Am I good or what?"

Chantel couldn't see anything through the thick mist.

"Who are you?" she asked in a quiet, shaky voice. She did not want to upset the hand that held her.

"I am a Rock Climber. I live in the cliffs of the Endless Gorge. What about you?"

"The last thing I remember is that I fell into a tunnel and slid out through a hole in the wall of the cliff," Chantel answered cautiously. She did not want to say too much.

"Oh yes, the tunnel. Lots of travelers fall into that trap. Some I catch; some I don't. But I think it is time to climb to the top of the cliff so that you can continue your journey."

Chantel nodded. "Thank you for catching me. I'm lucky that you were at the right place at the right time."

"No such thing as luck," the Rock Climber said. "Mother Nature told me that you would be coming, princess."

As they climbed to the top and came out of the mist, Chantel saw the Rock Climber for the first time. Like his hand, his entire body was composed of gray stones. His eyes were two white pebbles and his nose was a long pointy rock with giant craters for nostrils. When he grinned, his smile revealed two rows of white marble teeth. He blended into the cliff, and it was hard for Chantel to tell where his feet ended and the rocks of the cliff began.

"I have a very sensitive nose," the Rock Climber continued. "I can separate the nice creatures from the not-so-nice ones just by smelling them. I can smell the really evil ones, like Vampire Bats, from far away. You must have met some of them lately because there is still a slight scent of them on your clothing."

"Do you live here by yourself?"

"No," the Rock Climber replied. "There are many who are at one with the cliffs. We have been living here since the birth of the moons. I can still remember the time when only good smells floated across the Gorge, before the Evil One came. But now there are many rotten smells. Some of the

Rock Climbers have even plugged their noses with pebbles."

"Have any Rock Climbers sided with the Evil One?"

The Rock Climber looked insulted. Chantel was afraid his grimace would crack his face in two.

"I'm sorry," she said quickly.

"Don't be sorry. I shouldn't have expected you to know. No Rock Climber has ever joined the Evil One. Rock Climbers are lucky. Our good sides are as solid as our skin. So too are our beliefs. We are happy where we are and with what we are. Why should we look for more if we are happy? You, on the other hand, have a less solid foundation."

"I would never join the Evil One!" blurted Chantel.

"That's not what I meant," said the Rock Climber apologetically. "It's just that I can smell that you are restless."

"Yes, I guess I am. I'm looking for something." Chantel lowered her voice to a whisper. "I have to retrieve the relics."

"At least you know what you're looking for," replied the Rock Climber. "Remember, Mother Nature would never let you fall."

The Rock Climber moved swiftly and easily along the steep wall of gray. He and the rocks of the cliff flowed together like currents of a river. When he reached the top, he placed Chantel gently on a mound of grass.

"Thank you," Chantel said.

"To find the Wise One, follow the path over the hill and turn left. It's not far. I hope to see you again, Princess of Freedom." With a final smile, he turned around and climbed down the cliff. Before Chantel could say farewell, he was gone beneath the mist.

"Another friend," Chantel thought. "But where is Mouse?"

CHAPTER ELEVEN

The Attack

At the top of the hill, on a plateau that overlooked the entire valley, Chantel waited until dusk with the hope that the Wise One of the North would show himself.

But he did not.

She looked for a big tree and found one near the plateau's edge. She climbed to a big branch, curled up and quickly fell asleep.

In the middle of the night, she awoke to a shriek and the flutter of wings. When she opened her eyes, two yellow ones glared back at her. The Vampire Bats were back, just as Mouse had predicted.

"You again, wanderer," Brutus hissed. "Did you find your rocks or are you lost?"

"I haven't found my rocks yet."

"How did you cross the Endless Gorge?"

"I jumped," Chantel answered quickly. Too quickly.

"You jumped? Try again. Amuse me some more and you'll never find the rocks you desire."

"I . . . I built a glider and then jumped," Chantel stuttered. "The up-winds from the Gorge carried me to the other side."

"Well, like I said before, do not stray too far off your path, wanderer."

With that last threat, Brutus and his hoard of bats flapped away. The night became quiet again.

"Oh no," Chantel thought, touching her braid. "I didn't cover my hair!"

Filled with uneasiness, Chantel tucked her hair under her hood and tried to get some more sleep.

—✳✳✳—

The next morning, before the sun rose, Chantel paced the plateau, hoping to find the Wise One of the North, or at least some sign that he lived nearby.

"Could this be the wrong place?" she wondered. She walked to the farthest edge of the plateau looking for signs, but there were none. There was only a stream that fell down the plateau edge, creating a roaring waterfall similar to the one that had hidden the Magic Staff.

She took out the Staff and pointed the crystal at the sun. She tried to think powerful thoughts. Nothing. The Staff, so far, was useless. She put it away.

"Mouse would know what to do," Chantel thought. "I wish he were here."

Chantel heard a friendly "Hello" and tinkling laughter. She turned around. "Who's there?"

"Don't worry. It's just me. It is time to show myself." A girl, almost the same height as Chantel, emerged from behind a weathered bolder. She wore pink tights, a purple dress and ankle-high boots. Curly brown hair showed from under her hood. She had a small, pointy nose and a bright smile. Sticking out slightly from her back, but still folded, were two brown wings.

"Who are you?"

"Laluna. I am a Winged One," she answered as she turned around. Her wings unfolded like fans. Although they were brown and plain when they were closed, when open they were startlingly beautiful, like the wings of a butterfly, only much larger. Two circles, one red and one blue, like the night's two moons, graced the top half of each wing. Violet sprinkles covered the bottom halves. The wings were tissue-paper thin, and the sun shone through them, reflecting their colors and patterns across the ground.

"A Winged One?" thought Chantel. "Owl said they were all dead, destroyed by the red lightning bolt. Was he mistaken?"

"You don't have to worry about your friend, Mouse," Laluna said, taking Chantel's pondering look for concern. "He is fine. Mother Nature is just testing his loyalty to you, to the quest and to himself."

"Loyalty?"

"Yes. He needs to understand the self-sacrifice of a true friend, his commitment to his word, to his friends and to his family."

"How do you know all this?"

"Fin, the Wise One of the North, told me. I live with him in his cave. He rescued me from a wild boar that cornered me one moon crossing ago. The Wise One is gone now, but he will be back from his travels tomorrow," Laluna said. "The sun is traveling fast today, and it will be dark soon. The Vampire Bats will be back. One of them saw your Golden Braid."

"I know," said Chantel. "What should I do?"

"We can only hope that the bat hasn't passed on his knowledge to the Evil One. Most likely he has not. Vampire Bats are show-offs. He will probably gather his soldiers to kill you and then bring your body to the Evil One himself."

"That makes it better?" gulped Chantel.

"Better than the Evil One knowing of you, yes. The Vampire Bats aren't the most deadly creatures, but we will need help to defeat them. I have friends who have battled Vampire Bats before, but their village is far away. I must hurry and go to them now. You wait here and get ready for the attack. Don't bother hiding. Once Vampire Bats have locked on to a victim, they can sense it anywhere."

Laluna ran towards the weathered boulder at the edge of the plateau, jumped on top of it, spread her wings and flew away.

Chantel watched her soar into the clouds. Already she liked Laluna. "Maybe we will become friends," Chantel hoped and then puzzled once again over Owl's belief that all the Winged Ones were dead. "If one Winged One is still alive, maybe there are more," she thought.

⁓❦⁓

The sun was beginning to settle for the night, painting the mountains a wonderful, breathtakingly bright orange. Chantel followed Laluna's advice and prepared herself for what she thought might come. She covered her arms with bark from a willow tree, fastening it to herself with string from her pack. She sharpened her sword with a stone and practiced slicing leaves floating in the air. She also tried to use the Magic Staff again, but it did not work. "At least I can use it as a club," she thought.

When Chantel was as prepared as she could be, she sat on the weathered rock to wait for Laluna or the bats, whichever came first. Fireflies buzzed around the plateau, pinpricks of light in the increasing darkness. Stars began to appear in the sky, clustering brightest around the moons. She was calm and ready, although she wished that Mouse were by her side, even though he had failed to protect her before.

Suddenly chills ran down her spine. Her Golden Braid became heavy. Danger was nearing.

The air turned cold. The fireflies disappeared into the distance. They, too, seemed to sense the danger. Chantel looked up at the sky. It was black, the stars and moons blotted out by the swarm of descending bats. She pulled out her sword with one hand, clenched the Magic Staff in the other and crouched behind the boulder.

The wings sounded like a thousand snapping flags. Before she had a chance to blink, the Vampire Bats began to attack.

Chantel swung her sword and the Magic Staff furiously. Bat after bat fell lifeless to the ground, but bat after bat also ducked her sword and Staff and bit through her bark armor until it fell off in pieces. They began to bite her arms, shoulders and legs and even the top of her head.

Blood trickled down her forehead and into her eyes. But

Chantel did not give up. She continued to fight bravely, even as her strength drained away. She fell to her knees. Before she collapsed completely, she saw a tall, dark figure standing over her, swinging a giant glittering sword.

⚔

Chantel lay unconscious on the ground when Laluna returned. A hundred Fox Bats followed her, and at the Winged One's command, they swarmed the Vampire Bats. The sky was filled with flying creatures, and the air rippled out in waves from the beating of so many wings. The Vampire Bats and the Fox Bats fought viciously. Unbearable sounds—high shrieks of pain and agony—came from both bat armies. Commands came from all sides.

"Don't let those cowards attack the girl!" cried Laluna. "Fox Bats, my friends, fly down to protect her!" A swarm dove down to defend Chantel, who still lay on the ground.

The Vampire Bats' long fangs penetrated the necks of the Fox Bats, killing them instantaneously, while the long claws on the Fox Bats' leathery wings sliced through the Vampire Bats' bodies. The Fox Bats were stronger and faster. In the end, it was the Vampire Bats that dropped out off the sky like raindrops, forming lifeless black puddles on the ground. None of the Vampire Bats escaped, except cowardly Brutus. He had hidden behind a tree when he saw the Fox Bats approaching.

"I have to tell Aquila Bellum that I have found the one he is looking for, the one with the Golden Braid," thought Brutus as the last of his soldiers fell. "I will tell him in person so that I can collect the reward."

As quietly as possible, he flapped away unseen into the dark night.

"Once Aquila finds out, he will command all his helpers to find the girl and capture her. That will be the most triumphant day in the history of the Darkness, a day for celebration. It will signal the end of the prophecy and the end of the four lands." His grotesque face twisted into a smile as he began his flight over the Endless Gorge.

"Soon I will be the Evil One's most favored helper," he hissed. "Who cares that I have lost my army? When the Evil One finds out that I discovered the Last Descendant, I will be given a new army—a bigger one. With a bigger army and the Evil One's respect, nothing will stop me."

WHACK!

"Gotcha!"

A Rock Climber opened his hands and looked at the squashed bat. He wrinkled his big nose. "What a ghastly, disgusting smell." He turned his hands over and Brutus's lifeless body fell into the Gorge, twirling into the endless darkness, never to be seen again.

"I hate Vampire Bats," he said as he climbed down the edge of the cliff.

CHAPTER TWELVE

Mouse's Fight

When Chantel opened her eyes, she was lying on a small, white bed woven from thin branches of a willow tree. A blanket made out of thousands of cottonwood seeds sewn together floated above her like a cloud. It was incredibly light and yet so warm.

Her whole body hurt. Bandages covered her limbs and neck. She tried to sit up but fell back in pain. She carefully looked around, keeping her head on the pillow.

She was in a dimly lit room in a cave. Far away, as if in a dream, she heard Laluna's voice and a man's voice that was gruff and unfamiliar.

"She was very lucky today," said the man.

"I know," replied Laluna, "but she was quick with her sword and her Staff. Once she has learned how to use the power of the Staff, she will be able to defeat a thousand Vampire Bats by herself, just as you foretold."

"If I had known she was on her way, I would have been home earlier and all this could have been avoided."

Before Chantel could overhear any more of the conversation, a fog came over her eyes and she passed out.

⌐≡≡≡⌐

The next time she woke up, the room was quiet. A fire burned in the left corner of the cave. Through an opening in the wall, Chantel saw the waterfall. She tried to sit up.

"You fought bravely, young princess," Chantel heard the man say.

"Who are you?" Chantel asked, her voice weak.

"Do not try to sit up. Your wounds have not yet healed."

Chantel peered in the direction of the voice. A tiny bearded man sat in an old rocking chair beside the fireplace, smoking a long pipe. The walls of the cave behind him were covered with bookshelves, bending under the weight of many heavy books. To the left loomed a large wooden desk cluttered with glasses, vials and smoking apparatuses. The cave smelled like a strange combination of honey and grass. Perhaps it was coming from the smoking apparatuses, or perhaps it was the smoke from the man's pipe.

Laluna sat at the other side of the cave, at the top of a staircase that led to another level. She winked at Chantel. A bat sat on Laluna's leg, and she was caressing it.

"Don't be afraid," Laluna said when she saw Chantel's anxious expression. "This bat is my friend. He is an Epomops Franqueti, a Fox Bat. His name is Fox, and he hates Vampire Bats. It was his tribe that defeated the Vampire Bats."

"Hush," the man said to Laluna. "Chantel still needs to rest." The man rose from the rocking chair, set down his pipe and picked up a small cup from the table. He offered it to Chantel.

"Drink this, child," he said. "It will help you. The herbs in the tea will fight your fever and heal your wounds."

Chantel carefully swallowed the tea. The warmth of it bubbled through her body. When she was done, she set the cup on the floor and closed her eyes.

⁓❦⁓

Mouse was still sitting on the other side of the Endless Gorge when he saw the swarm of Vampire Bats flying overhead in the dark sky. He had been sitting there in a trance since Chantel had disappeared. He hadn't slept. He hadn't eaten.

As the Vampire Bats clustered in the distance, Mouse stared into the darkness of the Gorge, brooding over what had happened. He had failed Chantel three times and now she was gone, lost forever. "Why couldn't I change? What was I afraid of? Now Chantel is gone and we are all lost. The Evil One has won."

"Wake up!" a rough voice yelled at him. "What are you sitting here for?"

Mouse looked up and saw a large head at the edge of the Gorge. It looked like a big rock with bright crystals as eyes.

"Don't be so foolish. Get up! Chantel is on the other side and needs your help. Or are you going to fail her again?"

"Chantel's alive?" exclaimed Mouse. "How can this be?"

"Never mind. Just do what you are supposed to do: protect her!" the Rock Climber yelled.

Mouse paced along the cliff's edge. How could he help Chantel? There was no way across the Gorge. His frustration grew stronger and stronger. He stomped and shouted and kicked pebbles. He even picked up a twig that lay on the ground, broke it in half and threw it into the Gorge.

Then he had an idea. There *was* a way across!

"Change!" he yelled and jumped up and down. "Chaaannnngggggge!" He grew so mad that he lost himself in his anger and despair. He ran in circles until his wild side finally took over. He knew he was losing control, but he did not fight it. He had to help Chantel no matter what, even if it meant losing himself to madness.

He closed his eyes and tensed his muscles. His legs became longer. His muscles became larger, and when he opened his eyes again, they flickered yellow like the eyes of a wolf. His fur turned black and his little paws transformed into huge claws that held a massive, heavy sword.

Mouse was gone. In his place stood the Mighty Warrior.

The Mighty Warrior did not hesitate. He ran towards the Gorge, and with a giant leap, he flew off the edge and through the air.

THUMP!

His feet landed solidly on the other side. He crouched low for a while and listened. The noises of a battle drifted through the air: flapping wings, shrieks of Vampire Bats and Chantel's cries.

The Mighty Warrior ran, his long legs carrying him swiftly towards the battlefield. The ground under his feet vibrated, and with each step he kicked dust and rocks into the air.

He reached Chantel just as she passed out. Standing

over her like a shield, he whipped his sword through the air, slicing bat after bat. He swung his other claw through the air like a net, catching and crushing more bats like they were eggs and throwing their twisted, dead bodies to the ground. Filled with power and fury, Mouse stomped his feet and waved his arms. One of his hind legs almost kicked Chantel. Blood covered his face and sword. The beast within him tasted it and wanted more. He looked down and saw the white meat of a young girl, not recognizing that it was Chantel. He lunged to take a bite when his eyes caught the glint of a golden braid amidst the girl's brown hair. He stumbled backward, nearly dropping his sword.

Suddenly he heard a hundred more wings. He looked up and saw a Winged One followed by an army of Fox Bats.

He knew Chantel would be safe. These friends had come to help her. Turning around, he ran into a cluster of bushes and hid. Through the branches, he watched the end of the battle and the victory of the Fox Bats. Slowly he calmed down and changed back to his normal small self.

"No wonder Mother Nature separated us. I almost killed Chantel." Mouse was sad and disappointed with himself. He shivered and was afraid of the Mighty Warrior.

He desired so much to be with Chantel and to help her, but first he had to learn how to control the Mighty Warrior within him.

"Good-bye, Chantel," he thought. "We will be reunited again soon, I hope."

CHAPTER THIRTEEN

Eronimus Finsh

The next morning Chantel was able to get up. Her fever was gone, and although her wounds still hurt, the pain was dull, not sharp. Neither Laluna nor the mysterious man were in sight, but on the table near the fireplace was a cup of delicious tea, as well as a plate of toast and fried fish speckled with spices.

She drank and ate it all, the spices bursting on her tongue and sharpening her senses. She almost felt as if she were back at the castle with Owl. As she licked her fork, the little man came down the stairs.

She could see him clearly for the first time.

He was the same height as Chantel, with pointy ears like Laluna's. His hair grew in tufts behind his ears, and his beard was long and brown. He wore brown boots, green pants, a blue shirt and a dark red overcoat. "So many colors," thought Chantel. "He must like rainbows."

"Welcome to my cave," the man said. "I hope you are feeling better."

"Yes, thank you. Who are you? Where am I?"

"My name is Eronimus Finsh, but my friends call me Fin. I am the Wise One of the North."

"Oh! You're the Wise One! I've been looking for you! There's so much I want to ask you."

"Shh," hushed Fin. "Be calm, princess. You aren't fully healed yet. We will have many chances to talk."

Chantel looked over to Laluna and Fox, who were flying down the stairs. "Good morning," she said.

"Good morning!" replied Laluna.

As Laluna ate her breakfast, she described the fight and Chantel's rescue. Fin had arrived just after the fight was over. He had been collecting the flowers of a rare herb that only blossomed once a year.

"Has anybody seen Mouse?" asked Chantel.

Laluna shook her head.

Chantel quietly cleared the table, thinking about Mouse. When she was done, Fin, who was rocking in his chair, gestured for her to join him. A warm light shone through the waterfall, filling the cave with dim light. Chantel sat on the floor on a pile of moss.

"I will teach you about herbs and swordsmanship while you are getting well enough to continue your journey," said Fin. "I can also teach you about your Magic Staff. I can't train you how to use it. You have to figure that out by yourself, but I can tell you about its history and its powers. This depends on whether you want me to or not."

"Yes, please. I have so much to learn."

Fin nodded happily. He realized why Chantel was the Princess of Freedom. She was humble, and his senses told him that she was strong and true of heart.

"Come," said Fin. "First you must see my cave."

⌐╼₩₩₩╾⌐

Fin's cave was a maze of tunnels and holes. To enter it one had to crisscross through the waterfall, which fell down in different layers and particular angles known to only Fin and his friends. The cave was further protected by Kowalis, furry little creatures that cleaned the grounds in front of the waterfall and the plateau. They swept away all of Fin's tracks.

On the main floor of the cave was a kitchen, living room and fireplace. The solid rock floor was covered with red and green carpets made out of braided grass and herbs and cured in special glue made from willow tree sap. Round rocks of the same size and color of the floor surrounded the fireplace. Fin's rocking chair had a cushion made out of red moss, and the frame was built from rosebush branches. The rough walls were peck-marked with small nooks for candles.

The upper floor of the cave was one big room with two beds and many different sized desks. In one corner a small stream of water trickled down from the ceiling along a layer of moss that grew on the wall. Boxes, bins and bottles were carefully stacked in the other corners. Vials and baskets of spices and herbs and heaps of paper and notebooks covered the desks. The room smelled like a summer garden.

Every morning Fin taught Chantel and Laluna sword-fighting on the plateau. They spent their afternoons on the upper floor of the cave, learning about herbs.

Fin had a small leather-bound book filled with his herb and medicine knowledge that he carried in his pocket. Often late at night he would sit by the fireplace and write in it. Each page was dedicated to an herb, and Fin insisted that Chantel memorize all of them. There was agrimony, which was good for healing battlefield wounds; coriander, which was used to treat digestive ailments; fennel, which could clear lungs and heal coughs; and lavender, a soothing relaxant.

Chantel enjoyed living with Fin in his peaceful realm around the waterfall. "Were all places like this, before the Evil One awoke?" she wondered.

⚬⚬⚬

The Snow Walker paced impatiently across the high ridge above his cave. He had lost contact with Brutus. He took long strides, kicking at the snow and spitting at the birds. Brutus had told him he had met a wanderer who was looking for precious stones.

"Why didn't that stupid flying piece of leather tell me who the wanderer was?" he growled into his filthy beard. "I told him to look for a Golden Braid, but that idiot never pays attention."

His red eyes surveyed the mountain landscape. Everything was peaceful and quiet. "If only I had the Golden Sword. Then the Last Descendant wouldn't stand a chance," he thought.

His hands ached to touch the Sword again, to release its power and feel its strength and energy pulse through his veins. But finding the Sword had so far proven impossible. He had looked everywhere: on every mountain peak and every snowy plateau, in every cliff-side cave and every wooded valley. He'd even scaled the sides of the Endless Gorge. There were only three places he had yet to search: the huge lake in the middle of the three mountains, the highest mountain peak surrounded by the black thunderclouds, and the valley of avalanches, the home of the Avalanche People, a mountain tribe that had sworn its allegiance to the Evil One.

If the Avalanche People had the Sword, surely they would have given it to him or the Evil One, so it couldn't be with them. And he couldn't imagine that the Sword would be hidden in the huge lake. But then who was he to understand the logic of those who stayed true to their good side? The lake was closer to him than the highest mountain peak, so he decided to search there first.

"Soon, after I hear back from Brutus, I will dive to the bottom of the lake to see if the Sword is hidden there," he said, not knowing how close he was to finding what he so much desired. There was not much time left for Chantel to find it first.

CHAPTER FOURTEEN

The Staff's Colors

One afternoon, as Fin was about to begin a lesson on a new herb, Chantel caught a whiff of something familiar. She sniffed the air and walked over to a table that stood near the mossy corner of the upper floor. On top of the table sat a woven basket overflowing with white flowers.

"What are these?" Chantel asked.

"Those are the rare edelweiss flowers," Fin said.

Even though Chantel had never seen edelweiss before, somehow she knew its powerful scent. She knew she was connected to it, just as she was connected to the mountains. She closed her eyes and breathed in the fragrance deeply. She began to cry silently.

"What's the matter?" asked Fin softly. "Does it remind you of something?"

Chantel rubbed her eyes. "Do you know anything about my family, Fin?"

"I'm sorry, my child, I do not. But scents often invoke lost memories. Here, take some of the edelweiss. Perhaps it will help you in your search."

Chantel knew that Fin was not referring to her search for the Golden Sword. Gratefully, she pocketed a bunch of the white flowers. But as they began their day's lesson, she wished Fin would talk about that search, too. So far he had not said a thing about the Staff or the Sword.

One rainy morning her unspoken wish was granted. Fin decided to stay indoors rather than conduct the customary sword-fighting lesson. Chantel, unsure of what they were going to do, cradled her cup of tea and shot questioning glances at Laluna as Fin rocked silently in his chair. Chantel was about to ask if she could read one of his books when Fin leaned back in his chair and began to tell the story.

"I was there the night the boy held it. I brought the Golden Sword to the mountain gathering." His voice was soft, and Chantel and Laluna both leaned forward so as not to miss a word. "Nobody foresaw what would happen, but my people blamed me for not predicting it, for not protecting them. They thought I should have known of the Sword's evil side. That's why I live alone."

"Is the Golden Sword truly evil?" asked Chantel.

A funny look came over Fin. "I thought so when it released the red lightning bolt. But when I picked it up after the boy's hands had caught on fire, I could feel its gentleness and its goodness. Aurora, the head of the Mountain People's Council, will tell you more about the Sword when you meet her. She lives below the Lake of Clouds. I will show you the way there before you leave."

"The Lake of Clouds?"

"Yes," Fin answered with admiration in his voice. "It is a place where thick, blue clouds are trapped between three mountains. Few know this, but below the Lake of Clouds lies the City of Ice, where the last remaining Mountain People live in hiding. Aquila Bellum is trying to find their home because he knows that they have the Golden Sword."

"If Aquila was born and lived all his life in the mountains, how come he doesn't know about the Lake of Clouds?" Chantel asked.

"The Lake of Clouds was created only after Aquila left. Mother Nature spoke with the winds, and they pushed the clouds over the valley and formed the Lake of Clouds. Aquila does not know about that. He only sees a lake. But it is only a matter of time before he realizes the truth. If he finds the Golden Sword before you, Chantel, all will be lost. It is a very powerful weapon. But there is another powerful weapon . . . one you already have in your possession, one I know you've been thinking about . . ."

"The Magic Staff!" Chantel interrupted.

"Yes. You've been thinking about it even when you should have been concentrating on the herbs and our sword-fighting lessons." Fin chuckled.

Chantel gasped. "How did you know?"

"All four Wise Ones have special talents. I'm telepathic. I can read your thoughts, and I can send you my thoughts. You will find out with time the other talents the Wise Ones have. Now, let me answer some of your thoughts. The Magic Staff is for defense. It was never intended to be used as an offensive weapon. During the ancient times, before the Evil

One appeared, the Magic Staff was cultivated and raised by the Growers at the Rainbow Point, where water meets land in the West. The spirits of the four lands came together and agreed that the magic in the Staff should only be used to protect and help. They installed the four elements of the world in its crystal. The interaction of the four elements is influenced by the relationship between the two great life energies of love and strife. The bearer of the Magic Staff has to be true of heart and strong in mind. You are both; otherwise you wouldn't have been able to remove the Staff from the rainbow. The Protector of the Staff would have never released it. The four elements are:

Fire, represented by the color yellow.
Earth, represented by the color green.
Air, represented by the color indigo.
Water, represented by the color blue.

"All four colors are found in the rainbow and enshrined in the crystal. Now, listen closely:

Fire: Craving heat and warmth?
        Wrap yourself in blankets.
Earth: Hemmed in by steep walls?
        There is a ladder.
Air: Scattered by the wind?
        You will become whole.
Water: Swimming in invisibility?
        You will rise again.

"These are direct translations of the ancient writings. It took me many moon crossings to decipher them. If you think yellow, you can create fire. If you think green, doors will open and walls will move. If you think indigo, winds will rise to help. If you think blue, you will become invisible.

"That's what the ancient writings say, but no one has ever used the magic of the Staff, so be careful. Remember the colors and their powers."

"What about the remaining three colors of the rainbow that are also in the crystal?" asked Chantel. "What about orange, violet and red?"

Fin hesitated. An odd look crossed his face. Chantel's hair rose on the back of her neck. Something was wrong. "Is everybody hiding something?" she wondered.

"No, Chantel," Fin answered, "but not all can be revealed."

Chantel didn't understand. "Why not?" she thought. But this time Fin didn't reply. She watched as Fin started the usual procedure of stuffing his pipe full of special herbs. His hands shook slightly.

Finally he spoke. "The remaining three colors are the colors of the Evil One. For example, the lightning bolt of the Evil One is red. Although I studied the ancient writings for many moon crossings, I was unable to find any more information about those colors."

Chantel shivered. What was Fin hiding from her? What did he mean by "not all can be revealed"? She thought hard and looked into Fin's knowing eyes. Still, he did not respond to her mind's question.

Laluna noticed the tension building between Chantel

and Fin and asked, "Can the Staff produce a red lightning bolt like the Sword?"

"I believe so, but I'm not sure. The Evil One produces its own lightning bolts, and I've only seen the Sword replicate this power," said Fin, relieved that the silence was broken.

"But the red lightning bolt should not be your concern," he said, turning to Chantel. "Focus on the other powers of the Staff, the elements and colors that I have decoded."

He got up and put a copper kettle filled with water on a hook above the fire while Chantel sat mulling over this information. Laluna, too, was quiet, cleaning the tips of her wings with a cotton cloth. The water boiled quickly, and Fin poured it into a teapot, adding a sprinkle of lavender flowers. After a few minutes, he got three cups and poured the steaming tea into them. He passed one to Laluna and one to Chantel and kept one for himself.

"There is one last herb you must know about: rosemary," he said.

Chantel glanced at the open page of Fin's book.

> *Rosemary*: used to relax muscles, but when taken in large doses, it causes irritation of the intestine and cramps and can immobilize any enemy

⁘

The next morning, Chantel sat outside the cave on top of a weathered rock, looking at the moons. "Garlic is an insect repellant and wards off diseases," repeated Chantel from memory. "Fennel . . ."

"Hi!"

Chantel jumped.

"Sorry," Laluna said, crouching beside her friend. "I didn't mean to startle you. I've come to give you something."

"So I finally get to see what you've been up to." Every night, Laluna had been busy in her room and wouldn't let Chantel disturb her.

Laluna pressed a thin band into Chantal's hand. A small glowing stone hung in its center.

"It's a friendship bracelet. The stone in the middle is a rune stone, which I found years ago in an abyss near my village," explained Laluna. "These bracelets will always keep us together," she continued, her voice wavering as she showed Chantel a second bracelet. "They have magical powers. Whenever the two rune stone are apart, they stop glowing. To find the other rune stone, you have to lift your arm and point your rune stone in different directions until it begins to shine. We will always be able to find each other."

"Thank you," Chantel said. Laluna helped tie it around Chantel's wrist. Chantel tied the other one around Laluna's wrist, noticing Laluna's eyes fill with tears. When she was done, Chantel hugged Laluna, letting her weep quietly on her shoulder.

"What is it?" Chantel asked gently.

"My parents were killed when I found the rune stones. The rune stones saved my life."

Chantel wiped the tears off Laluna's cheeks and didn't ask any more questions. She knew that when the time was right, Laluna would tell her the whole story.

Chantel and Laluna spent the rest of the afternoon together, walking the plateau above the cave in a companionable silence.

Chantel finally spoke. "I sense it is time to leave. I feel strong and ready."

"Then I will, too," said Laluna.

"Are you sure?"

"I will not let you go alone."

The rune stones around their wrists glowed for a second.

Their conversation turned to less serious matters: the nature around them, their sword exercises and Fin's colorful clothing. When the sun began to set, they returned to the cave for a leisurely meal.

"Are the days shorter in the mountains, or is it just my imagination?" Chantel asked Fin as she finished the day's second cup of lavender tea.

"It's not your imagination. It's the influence of the Evil One. Gradually the days are becoming shorter and the nights are becoming longer. If the Darkness succeeds in overtaking the four lands there will be no more days—only night."

Chantel remembered Owl's words about the two moons going dark.

"So you'll be leaving tomorrow?" Fin asked.

"Yes," answered Chantel calmly, unsurprised that Fin knew.

⁓✦⁓

When Chantel woke up the next morning, she felt refreshed and eager to depart. Two packs filled with food sat on the kitchen table. Rolled-up blankets were fastened on top of the packs with leather straps.

"Are you sure you wish to leave today?" asked Fin.

"Yes, I feel strong enough, and I have to find Aurora. I have to find the Golden Sword."

"Very well," said Fin. "Follow the path beyond my waterfall that leads to the North. It will take you up into the mountains. From there you will be able to see the Lake of Clouds. You have to cross the snow-covered plateau before you reach the shore where the clouds meet the mountains. Walk down the hill, through the clouds. Below the clouds, you will reach a tunnel. On the other side of the tunnel you will find the City of Ice. Talk to the Mountain People and tell them you are the Princess of Freedom. They will lead you to the Golden Sword."

After Laluna said good-bye to Fin with a long hug, Fin turned to Chantel again.

"Remember," he said, "I am on your side, no matter what the future may bring."

"Thank you, Fin. Thank you for everything. Will I see you again?"

"I will be waiting for you at the castle." Before Chantel could express her delight, he continued, "There is something else I must tell you. Do not use the power of your Magic Staff too often or for too long. The power draws its energy from its user. Promise me."

"I promise," she replied.

When Chantel and Laluna, with Fox by her side, walked through Fin's waterfall, they were greeted by a spectacular sunrise. The clouds in the sky reflected orange sunbeams, and the air was fresh and welcoming, although a little chilly.

Fin watched them walk along the path that led north until they disappeared from view. A part of him wished he could go with them, but he had other important things to look after. He shivered and pulled his morning coat tight around his body. He turned around to walk into the warmth of his cave. He was looking forward to sitting beside his warm fire again.

"You can come out now," he said just before entering the maze of falling water. Behind him he heard the crackling of branches and the sound of small feet on stones.

CHAPTER FIFTEEN

The Rune Stones

The morning started out well. Fin's cave was nice and comfortable, but it was refreshing, almost giddying, to be on their way at last, traveling along the new path in the sharp, crisp air. By noon, Chantel and Laluna had reached the snow line, where the path became slippery and steep. The sun was high and bright, and their breath formed patterns in the air. Fox, on the lookout for enemies, swooped in and out of the clouds far ahead.

There were many cracks and rocks on their path, and Laluna kept turning around to make sure Chantel was okay. Sometimes when they reached an especially dangerous fissure, Chantel noticed Laluna touch her rune stone.

"Do you want to tell me your story, sister?" Chantel asked delicately after one such occasion.

After a while Laluna replied, "It happened when I was only four moon crossings old. I was walking with my parents not far from our village along the cliffs overlooking the ocean. It was my favorite place. The sunsets there were breathtaking, especially when the thunderclouds moved in from the open ocean and the sky flushed in hundreds of different shades of red, orange and violet."

"What colors?" Chantel interrupted.

"Red, orange, and violet," Laluna repeated.

"The three missing colors," Chantel thought. "Sorry for interrupting. Please continue," she said.

"I was busy practicing opening and closing my wings when I came to a crack in the rocks, a crack I'd never seen before. As I peered down it, I saw two stars shimmering at the bottom. I tried to reach them when all of a sudden the earth shook. The crack opened up, becoming an abyss, and I couldn't help myself. I tumbled forward and fell. My parents began to scream, but they were too big to fit down the abyss. 'Fly!' they cried. 'Laluna, fly!' I opened my wings and tried to fly up, but I was still too young and my wings were not strong enough. My open wings, however, slowed my fall and lessened the impact when I hit the bottom.

"When I opened my eyes, I was startled by two yellow lights. It took me a while to realize that I was looking into the eyes of a Fox Bat—my Fox's eyes. The two 'stars' were right beside me. They were two glowing rune stones, the ones on our bracelets.

"When I climbed up to the edge of the abyss, I was overwhelmed by what I saw," said Laluna. Her voice shook. "My parents were gone. The trees were gone, too, and all the houses of my village. The ground was black and smoldering as if a big fire had destroyed everything. But there was no fire, only a red light that danced across the land.

"Fox looked after me from that day on. He took me to his

village. His family taught me how to fly and find food. They gave me a new home." Laluna looked appreciatively at Fox, who had landed on her right shoulder. "What about your family, Chantel? You've never spoken about them, either."

"I don't know what happened to my parents," Chantel said. "I was raised by an old, gray owl."

"I remember an owl that used to live among us," Laluna said. "His house was in a large tree that stood in the center of our village. The owl was small with ghost-white feathers and an oval face. I can still see his warm, blue eyes winking at me. He was always present during our main celebrations and summer festivals. I remember one time he brought a shining star. I wonder if he managed to fly away or if he, too, died in the fire."

They continued their travels quietly. They gazed at the sky, the mountains, and Fox, who flew back and forth above them. From time to time, Laluna joined Fox. Chantel watched their graceful flight and was at ease. But as they continued to climb higher into the mountains, something began to trouble her senses. Her neck tingled. She turned around many times to see if anyone or anything was watching or following them. The forest was eerily still and silent. She tried to concentrate on the narrowing path, but she slipped from time to time because of her persistent premonition.

"What am I sensing?" she thought. "I know someone or something does not welcome us."

In a way, Chantel was mistaken. The creatures watching her indeed welcomed her. To them, she and her friends would be a delicious meal. The creatures turned around and made their way up the mountain quickly. Their broad feet carried them swiftly over the soft snow. They drooled at the thought of fresh human flesh and a dessert of wings, but first they had to inform their master, the Warlord of the North.

CHAPTER SIXTEEN

The Mighty Warrior

Mouse crept out from his hiding spot and followed Fin into his cave.

"Don't worry, young friend," said Fin, "your hiding spot was good, but my Kowalis are hard workers and good spies. They kept a close eye on you all the time. I know that you helped protect Chantel from the Vampire Bats, and I know why you want to see me."

"Can you help me?" Mouse asked.

"I don't know, but I will try. The good thing is that you came here seeking my help, and that you know what you want."

"Yes," answered Mouse, "I want to learn how to control my warrior self so I can protect Chantel."

"So tell me, what does it feel like when you change? Can you describe how you felt the last time you transformed?" Fin sat down in his rocking chair by the fireplace and filled his pipe. He took a burning stick from the fire and lit his pipe carefully. The cave filled with the pleasant smell of rum and plum. The smell and warmth helped Mouse calm down. Slowly, selecting his words carefully, he spoke.

"I felt like I was in a dream," Mouse said. "I saw what happened. I saw Chantel collapse. I saw the Vampire Bats attacking. I saw big, strong arms smashing the bats as if they were flies. What I didn't realize were that those arms were mine! I couldn't control what I was doing. I . . . would have attacked Chantel . . . if . . ."

Fin took a puff from his pipe and blew a smoke ring shaped like a four-leaf clover into the air. It drifted towards the cave ceiling, where it bounced once and lost its shape.

"From what you have told me, when you transform, your personality transforms as well," said Fin. "What do you remember from your past, when you were young and first transformed? Did the same thing happen?"

"No," said Mouse. "I used to change all the time when I was little. I used to be able to control it. Whenever I got hurt, I'd change so my bruises and wounds would heal faster. But I lost control on my thirteenth birthday. I don't know why."

"How did your family feel about your abilities?"

"They were afraid of me after that birthday. I accidentally destroyed our neighbor's den. I also hurt my brother."

"But what about before the birthday?"

Mouse shook his head. "I . . . I don't remember."

"Think."

Mouse put his paws on his head and thought as hard as he could. "They . . . they didn't like it. They always made fun of me. They teased me. When I changed everybody hated me. They called me a freak. So right before my birthday I made a vow that I would never change again. But on my birthday I changed even though I didn't want to. I tried to stop myself, but I couldn't. Instead I just lost control." Mouse grew pale. "Why did I forget that until now?"

"Sometimes when something awful happens to us, we suppress the memory of it," said Fin. "And sometimes when awful things keep happening, we suppress more than just memories; we suppress who we are. We change our memories, our behavior, our looks . . . we change with the hope that the terrible things will stop happening. But then we are no longer ourselves. You gave up on who you are because you did not want to be different from your brothers and sisters. And when you gave up on yourself, you gave up all control of your gift. You wanted to be loved and accepted by your family, but your family did not understand. They didn't know how to deal with you and your extraordinary gift. They were afraid and jealous. Mother Nature believes in you; otherwise she would not have asked you to protect and guide Chantel."

"But I failed Chantel three times and Mother Nature separated us."

"Mother Nature knows about your past. She knows about your pain and your hurt. She loves you, and that is why she sent you to see me. What you have to learn is that you must accept your special gift. Once you do, you will regain control of that gift that makes you who you truly are. You will become the true warrior you are supposed to be."

Fin got up and walked over to the kitchen table. He poured tea into his tiniest vial. "Here, drink this. It will make you feel better."

Mouse sipped the lavender brew slowly. He became tired and curled up on the kitchen table. Soon he was fast asleep.

Fin picked up Mouse and carried him upstairs. He put him carefully in a bed and covered him with a blue handkerchief he had made from the small, soft leaves of the morning flower. He returned to his fireplace and polished his pipe. He took the used cups to the kitchen, cleaned them out and put them away. Placing the red moss pillow from his rocking chair in the middle of his cave, he sat down and closed his eyes. He meditated for a few minutes to recover from the eventful day. Slowly his body started to float above the red pillow.

Fin had more than one gift.

CHAPTER SEVENTEEN

Trial and Error

The change from day to night happened quickly. Surprised by the sudden darkness, Chantel, Laluna and Fox searched for shelter. Without the sun it was very cold. Not even their fur-lined cloaks stopped them from shivering. They knew if they didn't find shelter soon, they would freeze to death.

But there was no shelter in sight. On one side was the steep slope that led to the valley far below. On the other side was the high cliff of the mountain, and in front of and behind them was the path.

Chantel held her Magic Staff in her right hand and remembered Fin's words. "Green represents Earth. Hemmed in by steep walls? There is a ladder. Doors will open and walls will move."

She thought about the color green and pointed the crystal towards the mountain. A green light shone from the crystal. The light lit up the snow on the rocks so that the snow looked like it was covered in moss. Her heartbeat quickened.

But when she moved the Magic Staff in a circular motion, nothing happened.

The cold mountain wind picked up, swirling snowflakes around their heads. Small droplets of perspiration formed above Chantel's lip.

"I can't do it," she yelled as doubt and fear crept into her mind. The crystal's light disappeared.

"Yes, you can," Laluna yelled back, against the noise of the wind. "Visualize what you are trying to accomplish."

The mountain wind became stronger and colder. Chantel's hair whipped across her face, and the perspiration on her face started to freeze.

She closed her eyes, filling her mind with green light and green memories.

Green smelled fresh, like peppermint, and looked like new grass in spring. Green tasted crisp, like lettuce and sour apples, and felt . . . what did green feel like? Like energy and growth. The crystal started to pulsate, and the green light appeared again.

When her mind was truly full of green thoughts, she began to imagine a cave in the mountain cliff. The Staff's power was very strong now, and it rushed through her body, feeding on her strength. She pointed the green light towards the cliff, and slowly the rocks crumbled to reveal a small hole in the mountain face. The power grew in her and spilled out the end of the Magic Staff. Her mind spun wildly, and she tried to find a way back out of the rushing flow of magic forces. It was as if she were trying to swim against the sea's most powerful currents. She couldn't fight it any longer. With a painful cry, she fainted into Laluna's arms.

When Chantel opened her eyes a few minutes later, she was inside the cave of her imagination, except now it was real.

Her head pounded, and her fingers still gripped the Magic Staff. They were blue and icy, and it took effort to pry them away from the wood. The wind wailed outside the cave, but now they were protected from the worst of the cold. But Chantel could not stop shaking. Her legs and arms were cramped and numb. Laluna gently wrapped a blanket around her and rubbed her limbs.

As Chantel rested, Laluna unpacked the meal that Fin had prepared for them. It was potato and spring onion soup, Fin's specialty, and it was still warm—perfect for their cold, hungry bodies. Carefully, Laluna fed Chantel, who was not able to hold a spoon. As the pain in Chantel's body lessened, she thought about the strength of the power.

"I underestimated how draining it is," thought Chantel. "I have to be more careful or it might kill me."

After they finished eating, the three of them huddled together and covered themselves with their blankets. Soon they were asleep, their dreams turning the howling storm into a distant lullaby.

CHAPTER EIGHTEEN

The First Encounter

When they woke up the next morning, the storm had stopped. The sun was still hiding behind the mountains in the East, and the air was very cold outside the cave. The storm had covered the path in new snow, which hid the icy patches and made traveling especially dangerous. Chantel and Laluna climbed purposefully, yet slowly and carefully, to keep themselves warm and safe.

After five hours of hiking, they reached the top of the pass and gazed down into a valley. The pine trees below them were covered with snow, as if the trees had been decorated in crystal scarves. Beyond the trees, towards the land of the West, Chantel and Laluna could see thick white and blue clouds trapped between three mountain peaks. The edges of the clouds rippled like waves. The clouds looked so much like water that if Chantel hadn't known the truth, she was sure she would have assumed it was a real lake.

"The Lake of Clouds," whispered Chantel. "We still have a long way to go."

As they walked along the mountain towards the lake, Chantel's neck started to tingle and her Golden Braid became heavier.

"Trouble," she said, stopping to look around. She did not hear or see anything alarming, but even so, she and Laluna grabbed the hilts of their swords. A slow, cold breeze was blowing down from the mountain pass.

As Fox flew higher to look for danger from above, Chantel and Laluna continued along the path. Chantel led with hesitant steps. None of them noticed the movement up the hill behind the broken pine trees.

Hidden in the shadows of the trees, a tall, muscular man watched every step the two girls took. His long, dirty fingers twitched with excitement.

He was not alone. Two huge wolverines growled quietly at his sides. They also watched the two girls eagerly, waiting for their master's command.

The man patted their matted fur gently. "You did well, discovering these travelers," he murmured. "They may be of some use. Soon you will have your feast, but first let me find out what they are doing here." Then he thought to himself, "Maybe they have some news about the Last Descendant. Eventually the Last Descendant will have to come to me, because the Golden Sword is in the mountains. But he will not leave with it, because it is mine."

Chantel felt eyes on her back. It was the same feeling she'd experienced the day before, but this time it felt worse, like the tips of long knives were touching her skin. She turned around, immediately spotting the large man with his two huge animals standing between two pine trees. Their eyes met, and the man was surprised that he was discovered so suddenly. He started to walk towards her, motioning for the two wolverines to stay behind.

"Careful, sister," Laluna whispered.

"I'm ready," Chantel replied.

"Don't worry," the man called out, waving at them. "I live here in the mountains. This is my home."

"Why should we be worried if you mean us no harm?" Chantel asked.

She disliked the man immediately. Two red scars ran across his face, and his black beard and long eyebrows were untrimmed and dirty. She could see the outline of a large sword under the right side of his fur coat. A bow and arrows were strapped across his back.

"Clever girl," thought the Snow Walker. "I mean no harm," he said, "but I've never seen two girls alone up here before, so far away from civilization. I assumed you must be lost and frightened. Is that not the case?"

"We're on a tour of the three mountain peaks," Chantel answered.

"All by yourself? No guides? No protection? How unusual. But then your company is quite unusual. A winged girl and a Fox Bat. Well, if you are on your way to the mountain peaks, let me walk with you. I know this area very well. I grew up in the mountains."

He took out his mountain horn and blew into it. The sound was hollow and sad, like the groan of a dying animal. The two wolverines howled and ran towards the girls and

Aquila Bellum. They growled, drool dripping down the sides of their mouths. Laluna clutched Chantel's arm.

"Don't be scared. These are my pets. They're harmless." Aquila smiled. He enjoyed his little game. He could sense the fear swelling up in the girls, and it gave him pleasure.

"I thought all wolverines were beasts of the darkness," Laluna whispered so only Chantel could hear. Chantel wasn't sure and shrugged.

Certainly the man was in total control of the two beasts. It was evident that they were afraid of him.

They walked together for a while, and the Snow Walker described his mountain world as he perceived it: dangerous and beautiful. He talked about avalanches, ice cracks, wild animals, weather changes and snow blindness. He explained the various words for different kinds of snow.

Chantel started to feel more comfortable, but her braid still felt like a string of stones. Although she was sure her senses were simply warning her to be wary of the two wolverines, she decided to stay on guard with the man, too. "He did not say the secret words, so he couldn't have been sent by Mother Nature," she thought, tugging her hood closer to her head.

The sun set quickly, and Aquila Bellum offered to share his shelter and food.

Chantel and Laluna gnawed on dried meat, watching Aquila build a shelter under a low-hanging tree. He skillfully bound some branches together with a leather string and constructed a wall of snow. "A little bit primitive for your taste, perhaps, but it will do for the night. The sky is clear. There won't be a storm tonight," he said.

"We will be fine," Chantel said quickly. "Thank you." She did not want to appear weak or helpless.

They settled down for the night. Chantel planned to keep one eye open at all times, but the long climb, the food, heavy in her stomach, and the hours of paying constant attention to the two beasts and the strange man led to the inevitable: Chantel fell into a deep sleep.

The next morning Chantel awoke to the sound of sniffing and growling.

Her neck hair stood up straight. Under her blankets, she made sure that both her Magic Staff and her sword were firmly in her hands. She could sense the two beasts were circling her and Laluna.

"Get up!" yelled Aquila Bellum.

Her eyes snapped open.

"You don't fool me any longer. I know who you are. I did not think you would arrive so soon, nor did I expect a girl. Ha! An innocent girl as the Last Descendant. Clever, but it will not make any difference when I kill you. I know what you are up to, but you will not succeed. The Golden Sword is mine. Get up! You will make a nice trophy, especially your Golden Braid."

She felt her head. Her hood had slipped off during the night.

"Fool!" she whispered. "Why didn't I learn from Brutus and the Vampire Bats?"

Laluna, who was up now, too, whispered, "Don't worry, Chantel. It was a mistake. I should have been watching out for you. Quickly, use your Staff. It's the only force we have that is powerful enough to defeat him."

"Him? Who is he?"

"He said, 'The Golden Sword is mine,'" whispered Laluna. "There is only one man that would say that."

"You're the boy who touched the Golden Sword," cried Chantel. "You awoke the Evil One!"

"So you've heard the old stories, little girl," said the Snow Walker, "and you think you know who I am. But do you know my pain or my struggles? I think not. But it doesn't really matter, does it? Soon you will be dead. Now get up and face me."

"Indigo," she thought. "Air, represented by the color indigo. Scattered by the wind? You will become whole. If you think indigo, winds will rise to help."

Chantel put the crystal of her Magic Staff under her cloak so its glow would not be detected. She thought about the many flowers Owl had planted along the castle wall. Their petals were a bright indigo. It was Owl's favorite color. She started to concentrate, but it was difficult. She remembered the painful exhaustion of using the Staff's powers the last time. She slowly stood up, her back to the Snow Walker.

"Turn around, girl," Aquila Bellum yelled. "I want to see your eyes when I kill you."

"You can do it, Chantel," Laluna whispered by her side. "You did it before. I am here with you."

Chantel let go of her fear and concentrated. She imagined the tall mountains and a great wind that would bring with it snow and rocks. She imagined the wind blowing the Snow Walker and his beasts away.

She was trembling when the power of the Magic Staff took hold of her. A force pulled her bones and blood towards the sky. She felt the drain on her inner strength, but she held on to the power and turned around. The crystal at the end of the Staff pulsated like a heart, and bits of the bright indigo light shone through the tears in her cloak. With a swift movement, she took the Staff out from under her cloak and pointed the crystal at the Snow Walker and his wolverines.

From the highest peaks of the mountain, a huge gust of wind rushed down with an angry scream. It hit the two wolverines first and hurled them into the air, carrying them away with the small shelter that Aquila had built the previous night.

Aquila Bellum's red eyes filled with anger and hate. He held his sword up high in his left hand and tried to walk towards Chantel, fighting the wind and power of the Magic Staff. He was determined to kill, but finally he, too, was picked up by the wind and flung into the air. "We will meet again," Aquila Bellum screamed. "Next time I will . . ." His voice faded away.

Chantel's legs buckled and she fell to her knees. She let go of the Staff. Her heart pounded wildly, and blood rushed through her veins. She lowered her head and started to vomit. Laluna held back her hair.

Chantel wiped her mouth. "I didn't faint this time," she said proudly.

Laluna gave her a weak smile.

Chantel kneeled for a while to regain her strength as Laluna collected their scattered belongings. Then they continued their hike towards the Lake of Clouds, quickening their pace. They didn't know where the Snow Walker had been blown to, and they feared they'd soon meet him again.

"What did he mean by calling me 'the Last Descendant'?" Chantel asked.

"It is written in the prophecy that the Last Descendant will come and face the evil ones," said Laluna. "You are the Last Descendant, Chantel. You are the Princess of Freedom."

"How can I be both? And what does being 'the Last Descendant' mean?"

"I don't know."

They continued their travels quietly. By late afternoon, they reached the mysterious shore of the Lake of Clouds.

CHAPTER NINETEEN

Another Encounter

Thick blue clouds swirled near their feet. They looked like small waves climbing up the mountainside. Chantel and Laluna inched their way down the hill. The clouds continued around their ankles, then up around their knees, and then around their waists. The girls didn't get wet, but when they were completely submerged in fog, they couldn't see a thing. "Take my hand," said Chantel. Fox clung to Laluna's shoulder.

Holding each other tightly, they continued downward. After ten minutes of walking, stumbling and sliding on the rocks, they broke through the other side of the clouds. Now the Lake of Clouds loomed above their heads. It looked even more magical viewed from underneath. It was as if they were walking under a canopy of billowing blue silk. A few stray sunrays sliced through the clouds, spotlighting the rocky ground. A giant rock loomed in the shadows in the distance.

As they continued they realized that the huge rock was no rock at all. It was a gargoyle.

Twelve feet tall, it had pointy ears, big eyes and a small pebble for a nose. "Like the Rock Climber," thought Chantel. Large wings rose from its back like stone archways. It was sitting in front of an entrance that led into a dark tunnel.

"We have to go through that tunnel to get to the City of Ice," Chantel said, remembering Fin's directions.

"Perhaps," replied Laluna in a whisper, "but we will not get past that monster. Gargoyles are mystical, mighty creatures. There are a few that stand guard and ward off unwanted spirits, but most worship the Darkness and are dangerous. I've heard that the ones with wings are the worst. They fly around at night to kill and sleep during the day."

"How do you know so much about gargoyles?"

"Fox told me," Laluna replied. "He is usually up when they are flying around, since he is a night creature, too. He said gargoyles can be as evil as Brutus—some even more so, because they're much bigger and stronger."

"Can we sneak by, or do we have to wait here until sunset, after he flies away? Do you think there's another entrance?"

"I don't know."

"Don't know what?" a loud voice bellowed.

Chantel spun around. The gargoyle stood no more than twenty meters away. His eyes rolled like pebbles in a landslide. He gnashed his teeth like flints being sharpened. In his hand, he held a long sword made of the same sharp rock as his teeth. He pointed it at them menacingly.

CHAPTER TWENTY

In Control

Mouse woke up the next morning well rested. He folded his blanket and placed it on the pillow. He thought about the previous day and Fin's wise words. "It's true that I've never liked myself," Mouse thought. "What if I were able to overcome my fears and accept myself for what I am? I'll be able to change into a strong, fearless warrior whenever I want to. What's wrong with that?"

"Nothing at all, Mouse," Mother Nature's voice echoed in the room. "Learn more about yourself. Learn to love yourself. After all, your true home is yourself."

Mouse kept on listening, but Mother Nature did not speak again. He hopped down the stairs and into the living room.

"Did you hear her?" Mouse asked Fin, who was eating breakfast.

"Hear who?" Fin asked.

"Mother Nature."

"No, I didn't. What she told you must have been for your ears alone."

Mouse walked out of the cave, nibbling some seeds from Fin's toast. He watched colors dance in the waterfall, letting a light spray of water dampen his fur. When he was done eating he zigzagged through the water to get to the other side.

On the same plateau where Chantel had sat the night before her departure, he sat and thought. In his mind, he traveled back to his childhood. His brothers and sisters were playing his favorite game: Race around the Crooked Tree. He allowed them to run ahead, and then he changed, running past them and leaving them in a cloud of dust. "Unfair! Unfair!" they squeaked.

His mind skipped forward to another memory. This one was horrible: the night his parents and neighbors came to kill him. At first he hadn't grasped what was happening. He saw it unfold again in his mind. He saw himself screaming and starting to run, and then he remembered the pain—not physical pain, but the pain of realizing that his parents were trying to kill him.

To understand why they did it, he had to hate his warrior self like they did. But he didn't really hate himself. It wasn't his fault that he was different. His head started to spin. Tears trickled down his cheeks.

As he looked up into the sky, he saw small, indigo-breasted birds dancing in the air. He heard their lovely songs, songs about freedom, happiness and the beauty of life.

"Accept yourself for what you are. Be the being you are supposed to be," he thought. He became calm and stopped crying.

He remembered the smiling face of a determined, brave young girl. He remembered the beautiful Golden Braid in her brown hair. He remembered her self-doubts. How could he, Mouse, convince her to believe in herself if he didn't believe in himself?

"Chantel is the one I have to protect. I am part of the prophecy. Our destinies are linked. Chantel, where are you?" he cried.

He jumped on top of the rock and started to concentrate. He closed his eyes and focused on his legs, his arms, his chest and then on his whole body. Sweat matted his fur.

He remembered how Chantel was excited and eager to see his warrior self and how she wasn't upset or appalled by it. Thinking about Chantel filled his heart with warmth.

A single sunray had worked its way through the layer of clouds and lit up the weathered rock. "Change," thought Mouse.

As Mouse's body began to grow, he concentrated on enjoying and accepting each change, even the pain that went along with the growth of his bones. His muscles stretched. His paws turned to claws. His fur darkened. It took a long time—longer than usual—but when he was finished, he was something different.

He listened and understood what he heard. The birds were singing. The waterfall was roaring. The bees were humming. And his heart was beating with excitement. He was able to think and see clearly and act accordingly.

He was in control!

"You did it," a voice called out. "No one could have shown you how. You found the way yourself."

Mother Nature appeared before him. Her dress was torn in places, its leaves brittle and dull. She looked weary, but she spoke with a strong voice. "Hurry now," she urged. "You have to find Chantel. She needs you."

Mouse changed back to his tiny self and ran through the waterfall and into the cave. Fin sat in his rocking chair, smoking his long pipe.

He smiled at Mouse and said, "This time I heard her, too. I have already packed your food."

"Thank you, Fin." Taking the pack, Mouse left the cave quickly. He was on his way to find the princess.

CHAPTER TWENTY-ONE

The City of Ice

Chantel held her sword and Staff in her hands. She knew she had no chance of winning against the huge gargoyle. She was still exhausted from using the magic power during the encounter with Aquila Bellum and too weak to call upon the Staff's powers again.

Laluna, noticing this, pushed Chantel gently aside and jumped into the air. She flew towards the gargoyle's head. The gargoyle moved swiftly, considering his size. He turned around to keep Laluna in sight. She circled the giant and tried to land on his head. With each step the monster took, the earth shook violently. Chantel lost her balance and fell.

When Laluna came close to the gargoyle's face, he opened his mouth and blew at her. She tumbled through the air like a leaf in a breeze. No matter how many times she tried to attack, the gargoyle simply blew her away. He seemed to be enjoying himself.

"Stop it!" yelled Chantel.

The gargoyle had forgotten about Chantel and turned

around to face her. He gave her a stony glare. Chantel took a step backward but didn't blink. They stared at each other for a while without moving until the gargoyle stepped even closer to Chantel. He knelt only a few inches away from her. He opened his mouth, revealing his teeth, which were sharpened to fine points. Suddenly his mouth curved into a smile.

"Enough of the game. It is time to introduce myself," he said in a friendly voice. The air vibrated with each of his words.

Chantel looked at him in shock, as Laluna landed by her side.

"My name is Norfalk, and I am the Protector of the City of Ice. Welcome Chantel, Princess of Freedom. I have been waiting for you."

Laluna raised her shoulders indignantly. "How could you?"

The gargoyle's gray face glowed like hot lava.

"I was just having fun. It gets so boring out here. I'm sorry." He looked at Laluna, hoping she would accept his awkward apology.

Then he turned to Chantel and said, "Few people can face my stare without blinking. You must be very brave and strong. The Mountain People have been waiting for you for a long time. Please follow me."

Chantel's anger dissipated, but Laluna, still disgruntled, whispered to Chantel, "Are you sure we can trust him?"

The gargoyle, overhearing this, knelt down again. "Please accept my apology, Winged One. You're an excellent flier. We should soar together above the mountains. I know that you would like the view, and I would like your company."

"You really think I'm good? I . . . I don't know sometimes," stammered Laluna. "I wasn't taught by Winged Ones, and sometimes I wonder if I fly too much like a bat and not enough like a Winged One. Not that that's a bad thing," she added quickly for Fox's sake.

"I've seen many Winged Ones in my youth," said Norfalk, "and you fly like the best of them. You also must be very special. I've never seen a Winged One with such beautiful and colorful wings."

Laluna beamed. "Thank you," she said with a smile. She had forgiven the gargoyle.

"Norfalk and the Rock Climber are quite similar," thought Chantel. "Such destructive-looking creatures with such gentle voices and polite manners."

"The City of Ice and the Mountain People are on the other side of this rock face," said Norfalk, ducking into the tunnel that his huge body had blocked before. Chantel and Laluna followed. The tunnel was just wide enough for Norfalk to crawl through on his knees and hands, but Chantel and Laluna were able to walk without having to stoop. The rock walls were smooth and the floor glowed with a mysterious yellow light that lit their way.

"The light is coming from the lava rivers far beneath the rock floor," Norfalk explained. "It took many hands and many moon crossings to chisel this passage into the mountain."

Norfalk continued for a long time. Finally they spotted a dazzling white light emanating from the tunnel's end.

"Welcome to the City of Ice," Norfalk said triumphantly, reaching the opening. "I must leave you now. Do not worry. You are safe here. I must return to guard the entrance." With a final wink and a whisper, he said, "Please don't tell Aurora about the games I played. She wouldn't understand."

Norfalk turned around and crawled back into the tunnel, leaving the three travelers to enter the city alone.

Chantel, Laluna and Fox gasped in awe. They were standing in a huge cave at least thirty times larger than Chantel's castle and hill combined. Inside the cave stood a snow-white castle with hundreds of towers, windows and balconies. The tower cornices were adorned with sculptures, such as elegant white swans carved from ice, and on the tip of the topmost tower, an ice star glittered like a giant jewel. Above the star, the top of the cave was a huge ice dome that spread out like a white sky.

Chantel and Laluna faced a large gate in the wall that surrounded the castle. Ancient symbols and letters were engraved into the gate's frame, and mounted across its top was a sword carved in ice. A red ruby sparkled in the middle of the sword's hilt.

Chantel heard chanting and singing. The gate slowly opened inwards with a sound like ice breaking. Through the open gate, Chantel and Laluna could see the gardens that surrounded the castle. Trees, flowers and bushes were all carved from glittering ice. In the garden stood a group of tall people dressed in white robes that shimmered like the ice sculptures. They approached Chantel and Laluna, their voices rising and falling in harmony. White birds with long, blood-red tails dipped in and out of the crowd, adding their low trumpet-like cries to the song. Smaller birds with blue-tipped feathers cheeped like the tinkling of spoons hitting crystal glasses.

They were singing the ancient welcome song of the Mountain People.

Chantel sighed as a feeling of warmth burst in the pit of her stomach.

The crowd stopped a few paces away from Chantel and Laluna. An elderly lady wearing a crystal necklace moved towards Chantel. Her silver hair was braided into three ropes held together by a golden ring at the back of her head. Her dress looked like it was made of strings of snowflakes stitched together. It was as silver as her hair. She smelled like edelweiss flowers.

"Welcome, my child. We have been waiting for you. It is time. My name is Aurora." She held out her hand. Chantel took it and was surprised by its warmth. She let Aurora lead her through the singing crowd.

As they moved forward, the people stopped singing and knelt down, bowing their heads. Chantel could hear their whispers: "A girl." "She's so young." "This cannot be right." "We can't give *her* the Golden Sword."

She did not pay any attention to what was being said. She understood their surprise. She still had doubts herself about her abilities.

Aurora stopped in front of a crystal sled. She stepped into the back, gesturing for Chantel and Laluna to follow. When they were seated on soft cushions, the sled lifted up into the air and began to fly towards the castle.

As they soared high above the ground, Chantel looked below and gasped. "It's so beautiful."

"It may be beautiful, but many of my people see it as a prison. It is, after all, not our true home, only a refuge from the Darkness.

"We have lost many people to the Evil One. Some have

been killed; others have gone to it willingly. You have met one of them: Aquila Bellum. The Evil One helped him survive after he touched the Golden Sword. It manipulated his mind and values. You were fortunate to escape your encounter with him."

"How did you know about . . .?"

"My mountain birds told me," said Aurora. "But the time for this talk will come later. You must be very hungry and exhausted."

The sled swerved around the castle's towers, alighting on the balcony of the tallest one as gently as a snowflake. Aurora raised a hand and the balcony doors opened.

The air inside the castle was crisp and fresh, but Chantel and Laluna didn't feel cold. Warm lights glowing from the ceiling played with Chantel and Laluna's shadows on the white floor. Fox flew around happily. Aurora led them into a room with three large wooden tables. Many beautiful ice carvings and crystal sculptures decorated the top of one table. On top of another were strange-looking musical instruments: a giant wooden horn, a flute that looked like it was made of ice, and a stringed instrument shaped like an octagon. On the third table were a stack of parchment and quills.

"This is our art room where we teach our children the ancient trades and skills. Here they also learn to sing our traditional songs and play our ancient instruments. Please sit down and make yourselves comfortable."

Aurora departed, leaving Chantel and Laluna alone in the room.

"What a beautiful place," Laluna said, "but I wouldn't be happy if I lived here all the time. I already miss the sun."

"And the mountains and the moons," added Chantel. "But I would rather live here than outside under the constant threat of the Snow Walker and his beasts."

Aurora returned with some chilled peaches and warm bread with goat cheese. While Chantel, Laluna and Fox enjoyed their meal, Aurora stirred and sipped a frosty drink. When they were finished, she led them into another room where two comfortable beds stood along opposite walls. The walls were painted with mountain scenes showing high peaks, blue lakes and grassy meadows.

"Good night. Have a good rest. I will see you tomorrow, and we will talk then."

"May I ask you one question now?" Chantel asked.

"Yes, of course."

"Why do some call me the Last Descendant and others call me the Princess of Freedom?"

"You are both. Mother Nature gave you the name Princess of Freedom because you will be the one who will set us free. But in the prophecy you are described as the Last Descendant. What it means exactly, I don't know, but I am sure you will find out. Now get some rest. Tomorrow may bring many challenges."

⟶✦⟵

As soon as Laluna snuggled under the warm blankets, she fell asleep. Fox perched upside down on the crystal chandelier and started to snore immediately. But Chantel couldn't sleep. "Many challenges?" she wondered. "What did Aurora mean? What could they be?"

CHAPTER TWENTY-TWO

For Us to Share

The next day began with a huge breakfast in the main dining hall. Crystal chandeliers hung from the high ceiling, and hundreds of small, silver gargoyles with outstretched arms mounted along the walls held burning candles. The main table looked like a small mountain range with heaps of goat cheese cut into tiny triangles, stacks of chilled sausages and salami, and baskets bursting with steaming freshly baked dark bread. There were bushels of grapes the color of emeralds and gold bowls filled with red plums, pink onions and green flowers. There were little bowls of nuts and squares of dark chocolate. Everything looked delicious and smelled wonderful.

Many dignitaries joined in the feast. Although they greeted Chantel with smiles, their eyes were cold, and they watched the girls' every move. Chantel started a conversation with an old man sitting across from her, but he gave short answers to all her questions. She felt so uncomfortable that she could only nibble a bit of cheese and bread.

At last Aurora got up, excused herself and her guests, and led the girls into a more private room in one of the towers. The walls of the small room shimmered in many colors, as if they were illuminated from the backside.

"Eight corners, just like my tower," Chantel observed.

"Yes, it was one of Fin's ideas," Aurora explained. "Although he helped design this castle many moons ago, he chose the life of a hermit instead of living here with his people."

"That's not what Fin said. He said that the Mountain People didn't want him to live with them."

"Not true," Aurora replied, to Chantel's surprise. "He blames himself for what happened even though no one could have known about the dark power in the Golden Sword. He was brave enough to take the Sword after Aquila dropped it and return it to your castle and later retrieve it so it could be hidden with us here."

"Why was it taken from my castle?"

"The story of the Golden Sword must be told from the beginning," said Aurora. "Please, seat yourselves comfortably."

Laluna curled up in one of the large crystal chairs. Fox perched on her shoulder while Chantel sat on the soft carpet woven out of sheep's wool dyed with red and blue mountain clay. Aurora took a seat in another crystal chair.

"Where do I start? The ancient writings only explain part of what happened. There is only one book that contains all the knowledge and all the truth. It is *The Book of Erebus*. It is kept in a secret place. Few have ever read its pages. Those who have the sight know where it is and are allowed to write in it. Erebus, the oldest and wisest of the ancient ones, originally began writing this book. Before his death, he passed the unfinished manuscript on to the next one who had the sight. That one, in turn, passed it to the next one, and so on. From what I know, the last one with the sight who was allowed to write in the book was living with the Forest People.

"I have not read the book, but I do know most of the history of the Golden Sword. A long time ago—eighty-five moon crossings to be exact—the Spirit of the West called for a council meeting between the spirit world and the human world. All four spirits were present: the spirits of the East, the North, the South and the West. The creatures of the lands were represented by the four Wise Ones. Mother Nature was there, too. The Spirit of the West was troubled. There were problems in her land, and something had to be done. After days of discussion, the council decided to forge four relics, one for each of the four lands. The relics were designed to represent the values of the humans. They were created to remind the humans of their good side."

Aurora looked at Chantel and Laluna and saw that they were listening attentively. Chantel's eyes shimmered with excitement. Finally she was learning about the important events that had happened so long ago.

"The Golden Sword was forged by the ancient blacksmiths of the North, who had the skill of wielding the light power. Mother Nature provided the materials that were needed. She gave the blacksmiths gold from the lost mountain's rivers and creeks. She gave them fire from a forgotten tunnel of an old volcano. She gave them the sand from hidden riverbanks to make the mold. One night, under the watchful eyes of Mother Nature, the four spirits and the four Wise Ones came together in the North to bring the Golden Sword to life.

During the life-celebrating ceremony, sparks flew from the Sword and the phrase "For Us to Share" was engraved by magic on the sides of its blade.

"For years the relics did their job. Then, fifty-five moon crossings ago, a powerful warlord came to reside in the West. The Spirit of the West was rightfully worried. Nobody knows who that being was, but it killed the humans in the West and then started to kill humans in the other lands, too. It may have even killed the Spirit of the West herself.

"The Evil One, as we named it, could only be stopped through a final confrontation, the Great War, between the Evil One and the Wise Ones, the spirits and the creatures of the four lands. After a long and terrible battle, the Evil One was defeated and banished from the four lands to an island, where it was chained and put into a deep sleep—a sleep that was supposed to last forever. A search for the Spirit of the West began immediately, but she was never found.

"Time passed again in peace. The relics were put in your castle for safeguarding, and brought out once a year to remind the humans of their values and to celebrate life and harmony. The Golden Sword was supposed to remind the people of the North to share. Slice your bread and share it with those who are hungry. Slice your cloth and share it with those who are cold. No one knew that within it hid a dark power.

"But when Aquila Bellum touched the Sword and released evil, Fin and I realized that the Spirit of the West must have planted dark power as well as light power into the relics. I believe that when the relics were first forged, she didn't trust only light power to protect her land. Unfortunately, it is this dark power that has caused the problems we face now, for it has awoken the Evil One, and now it is only a matter of time before the Evil One shows itself."

Aurora stopped for a few minutes to collect her thoughts and then continued. "Soon after Aquila touched the Sword, he returned to our village and killed many people. We fled to this valley, and Mother Nature called upon the winds and clouds to hide us, much like how she has hidden your castle, Chantel. We hid here, hoping we were wrong, that the Evil One had not awoken. But when the village of the Winged Ones was destroyed with a red lightning bolt eight moon crossings ago, we knew the Evil One was indeed awake."

"That was when my parents were killed," Laluna said softly. Chantel went over to Laluna, putting her arm around her sister's shoulders. Laluna was shaking.

"We are not sure why your village was destroyed and your family killed, Laluna. The four Wise Ones, Mother Nature and I had a meeting. We agreed that the relics must be taken from the castle and hidden in their respective lands. It is part of the prophecy found in *The Book of Erebus*. Look."

Aurora pointed to one of the walls of the room where these words were carved into the ice:

> **When the Evil One returns, the red lightning bolt will be the sign to retrieve the four relics from the house of the Last Descendant. Hide the relics from the Evil One and the Last Descendant as well, since the Dark Side tempts all. Until the Last Descendant passes a test and proves worthy to carry the relics, do not give them up.**

"The Mountain People still believe in the power of the Golden Sword and hope that one day it will kill the Evil One and Aquila Bellum, but the Golden Sword in the hands of Aquila Bellum would guarantee the fall of the four lands. He would use the red lightning bolt to destroy everything."

"So the Golden Sword is here in the castle?" Chantel asked, surprised.

"Yes. It's hidden in a protected hall."

They were quiet for a while.

"You were present when the Aquila Bellum touched the sword, weren't you?" Chantel asked.

"Yes. I witnessed the change in the boy. A hero one minute, an enemy the next."

"Do . . . do you think that will happen to me if I touch the Sword?" Chantel asked, remembering the hatred in the Snow Walker's eyes.

Aurora stood up and placed a warm hand on her shoulder. "I dearly hope not. I doubt it will, because, as the prophecy states, before we can give you our precious belonging we have to test your worthiness. Today you will meet Noctambulant, the Sleepwalker, the one who will test you."

"When?" asked Chantel.

"If you wish, we could go there now," said Aurora.

Chantel nodded.

"Very well. Come with me," said Aurora, leaving the room. Chantel and Laluna followed her.

"Not you," Aurora said to Laluna. "Chantel has to meet the Sleepwalker alone. Wait here for us; we will return soon."

Chantel gave Laluna a quick wink before turning to join Aurora. She wished Laluna could go with her.

Aurora led Chantel through the castle, through many halls lined with windows and mirrors. The window frames were carved carefully into the ice, showing scenes of wild boar hunts and people dancing around huge fires. The supporting columns were engraved in a pattern of crisscrossed lines. The windows themselves were painted in frost.

They walked quietly side by side until Aurora stopped in front of a very smooth ice wall. Chantel looked at her in surprise. "Where is the door?" she thought.

As if Aurora could read her mind, she smiled and took out a very tiny object from her pocket. Chantel peered at it closely. It was a golden key the size of a baby tooth. Deftly, Aurora scratched some ancient symbols in the flat wall. A massive wooden door with iron hinges appeared where the ice wall had been. Aurora slipped the key back into her pocket.

There were many signs and symbols engraved in the wooden doorframe. Some looked like headless bodies; others looked like praying birds. Chantel could see a sword engraved in the top right-hand corner of the door. From its tip, lightning bolts zigzagged across the door to the lower left-hand corner, ending in the palm of a boy's outstretched hand.

"This is it," Aurora said. "This door and the chamber behind it were designed by the ancient Wise Ones with the help of the light magic. Only the right one will pass the test of the Noctambulant. I do not know what will happen on the other side of the door because I have never gone through it. Those who were not supposed to enter the chamber have never returned."

"How do you know that I am supposed to enter?" Chantel asked.

"I don't," Aurora replied, "but you have the Golden Braid as prophesized. You carry the Magic Staff, and you found us. These are all indications that you are the right one. The Noctambulant will know for sure. My blessings go with you." Aurora kissed her lightly on the cheek.

Chantel took a deep breath, opened the door and walked into a dark room. The door closed behind her with a soft thump.

⁓⧟⧟⧟⌐

The trees and shrubs flew by as the Mighty Warrior ran up the hill, following the path that Chantel and Laluna had taken several days before. His strong hind legs carried him swiftly up into the mountains. It took him only a day to reach the spot on the cliffs that overlooked the Lake of Clouds.

The high peaks, surrounded by white clouds, made him feel very small. A voice within him told him to wait there until he was needed.

The Mighty Warrior changed back into Mouse and scurried into a small cave in the mountain face. From its entrance, Mouse could look at the lake without being seen. He still remembered the shame of not being able to protect Chantel when she was pulled into the waterfall while trying to retrieve the Magic Staff. He had to make her believe in him again. He walked out of the small cave and practiced controlling his gift. He changed back and forth from Mouse to the Mighty Warrior. At first it took him much time and concentration, but after the thirteenth time, he could change within the blink of an eye. He was ready to protect Chantel. He was Mouse, the Mighty Warrior!

CHAPTER TWENTY-THREE

The Noctambulant

To test your strength of mind and spirit, you must walk in the mists of time. The Sleepwalker awaits you there. Who is the Sleepwalker? The Sleepwalker is constructed from one's own imagination, one's own fears and doubts. No wonder the Sleepwalker is considered by many to be one of the deadliest of enemies.

From The Book of Erebus

The chamber was empty and cold. A heavy fog, the same kind that made up the Lake of Clouds, engulfed the room, making it impossible for Chantel to see farther than the tips of her fingers on her outstretched arm. Chantel stood motionless for a while, but nothing happened. She took a few careful steps forward.

"Welcome." Two familiar red eyes appeared in front of her.

"Aquila Bellum!" Chantel started back in horror as the man's body formed around his eyes. "It can't be. It's a trap. AURORA!" she cried. She turned around, but the door behind her had disappeared.

"You got rid of me so quickly last time that I couldn't tell you about the Darkness and how beautiful it is," said Aquila, his voice as sweet as honey. "The Darkness takes away your worries and cares. It lets you think about yourself and not about others. You are important. If you want something, just take it. Look after those who suffer? Why? It is a waste of time. Ignore them. Walk right over them and take what you want. Those who sent you on your quest complain about the Darkness. They warn against greed and desire for power. But look at them. They sent you to retrieve silly relics. They expect you to give up your life so they can enjoy theirs again. Isn't that selfish—sacrificing a young, innocent, brave girl for their own gain? Why don't they complete the quest themselves? They told you that you are the one who will save them. They told you that only you are strong enough to retrieve those cheap relics that have no power. Isn't that what they told you? How do you know they speak the truth?"

Although Chantel knew that Aquila was trying to trick her, she couldn't help but listen. "I *was* sent by others," she thought. "It was not my idea to go on this journey. Why does the Snow Walker sound so convincing?"

"And what about your parents? I know you believe that they are still alive."

Now Aquila Bellum had Chantel's full attention.

"My parents! What do you know about my parents?"

"I presume they have not told you," replied Aquila. "They just left you alone to guess. On the other hand, I am real, and I will not leave you guessing. I will show you the good side of the Darkness. If you decide to listen to me, I will never leave you. I won't send you strangers who are supposed to help you and then disappear and fail you."

"What about my parents?" Chantel yelled. "What do you know about them?"

"Ah, parents," he sighed. "I killed mine. That was the price I had to pay to prove my loyalty to the Evil One. The Evil One gave me strength and power. All I need now is the Golden Sword."

"You will not get it! I will make sure of that."

Aquila smiled. "Are you really so sure, Chantel? Do you think you will be able to wield the Sword? I have held it before. I know how powerful it is. I have the power now to touch it again, and it will obey me. I can teach you about the Sword. I can help you."

Chantel didn't know what to do. She started to run.

"That's right, Chantel, run! Run so they can't find you and bother you anymore. Run, Chantel, run!"

Chantel sped deep into the thick fog. The sound of falling water grew louder and louder until she reached a large cave beside a roaring waterfall. The fog cleared enough for Chantel to see inside the cave. On the ground lay a woman. Her face was white and her eyes were closed. Another woman standing beside her cradled a tiny baby wrapped in a pearly blue blanket. Suddenly the baby began to wail. A burst of light and stars surrounded the lifeless woman. Chantel watched in awe as the body of the mother transformed into a creature covered with silvery white fur.

Before Chantel could speak or move towards them, she heard Aquila's voice: "Run, Chantel, run!"

Fog obscured the cave entrance, and although Chantel desperately wanted to know what was happening in the cave, she turned around and fled away from the waterfall, and back into the fog.

She heard the familiar hoot of an owl. Something red flashed in the mist in front of her. The red thing passed by again, and this time she could make out what it was—Fawn! He was flying through the air like a ghost. Then Chantel realized Fawn wasn't flying; it was the creature holding him—Owl!

"Owl!" cried Chantel. "What are you doing?"

Before Owl could respond or Chantel could reach out to Fawn, Aquila's voice yelled again, "Run, Chantel, run!"

Again Chantel obeyed, running through the fog down a path and into a valley, trembling from what she'd seen and how she felt. She tripped over a root and fell down. When she stood up, she noticed that the trees around her were brown and dead. The grass was dead, too, and there were no creatures in sight. No animals moved, no birds flew, no humans walked. Other than the skeleton trees, which were tinted red, it was a bare, surreal landscape. She looked up to see the two moons in the sky. They were both dark blood red. Where was the silvery blue moon? Was this a vision of the world under the Darkness?

"It cannot be!" whispered Chantel.

"RUN, CHANTEL, RUN!" screamed Aquila from the foggy path.

"NO!" yelled Chantel. "I will not run anymore!"

"Don't surrender, Chantel," she told herself, turning around. "Do not surrender. You know what's right and what's wrong. You are stronger than Aquila Bellum."

As she muttered these words over and over, a sword as bright as the sun appeared in her hand.

"No!" Aquila Bellum screamed. "The Darkness will rule the world, and you will not stop it, not even with the Golden Sword!" Aquila Bellum's shouting faded into the distance, and with it, the Golden Sword faded from Chantel's hand.

Chantel stood still for a moment in the lifeless land. She focused, reviewing in her mind what she had just experienced, and then she knew the meaning of all her visions.

"I don't have to run any longer. I will not accept this future. I know who I am," she said. Thinking about Aquila Bellum, she added, "And if *you* don't know by now, just watch me. I am the Princess of Freedom, and I am the one who will free our lands from all the evil harming us."

All was quiet again, and the dismal valley disappeared. Chantel was back in the indigo fog.

"Sorry for what just happened," Chantel heard. She saw the outline of a person through the fog. The figure was of her height and build. She leaned forward, squinting.

"Don't try, Princess of Freedom," said the figure. "You will not be able to see me. I am the Sleepwalker and this is my chamber."

"You're the one that created all those things?" cried Chantel. "The cave and Owl and Aquila?"

"Yes and no," replied the Sleepwalker. "All the images you saw were created by you, in your imagination. They were your own doubts and worries and maybe some of your lost memories. I only made them come to life. I had to test you because you want the Golden Sword, and Aquila Bellum will do anything to get it. You can't allow that to happen. Once the Mountain People give it to you, you have to return it to your castle and place it into its protective spot as quickly as you can. The Darkness is so strong this time that only the combined powers of the four relics will save the four lands. Do you understand this?"

"Yes, I do," replied Chantel. "Do you know about my parents?"

"They are no longer alive. I am sorry, but do not give up. Now go."

Chantel stood motionless for a few minutes. "So they're dead." Tears began to stream down her face. "Now I know. They're dead."

"Do not give up," repeated the Sleepwalker. "Remember, you are still in the chamber. All you hear in here is born of your own fears."

"Aquila Bellum killed his parents," thought Chantel, remembering his words. "There is a connection among him, the Evil One, the Golden Sword and my parents. I know it. I feel it. I hate Aquila Bellum. I will find all four relics and set us free again. I promise this to my dead parents. I will be strong and fulfill my quest. I am the Princess of Freedom. I will make them proud of me."

Suddenly a door opened and she could see a light in the distance. She walked towards it through the fog and passed the place where she'd heard the Sleepwalker's voice. There in the mist she could see two blue eyes—exactly like her own—and they winked at her.

"Believe and you will find what you seek."

Then she was alone again. She continued towards the light and the opening in the wall and stepped out. The chamber door shut behind her. She was back in the hallway, where Aurora stood waiting.

CHAPTER TWENTY-FOUR

A Message or a Warning?

Chantel couldn't stop trembling. Taking her hand gently, Aurora led her down the hall. "I know a wonderful place where you can rest," said Aurora. "Come."

Aurora supported Chantel, and together they walked through the castle and came to a room with a giant bath. Steam rose from the bath in thin tendrils, and small star-shaped flowers floated in the water and filled the air with a sweet aroma. Laluna was already in the water, her wings splashing and keeping her afloat. "Oh, I'm so glad you're safe!" she exclaimed.

Chantel undressed quickly and joined Laluna.

"I will get you something to eat and warm nightgowns," Aurora said and left the room.

Chantel and Laluna quietly enjoyed the warm water for a while. Laluna didn't ask about Chantel's experiences in the chamber. She waited patiently.

Once Chantel was fully relaxed, she began, "It was awful. I started to doubt myself, Owl, Mouse, you and the quest. I almost lost myself to the Darkness, but I didn't let it happen. I was strong." Chantel paused and then added in a sad voice, "I also found out that my parents are dead."

"Oh, Chantel, I'm so sorry." Laluna gently touched Chantel's shoulder. "How did you find that out?"

"The Sleepwalker told me," Chantel answered. "I saw her."

"What did she look like?"

"A girl just like me. Well, I think it was me, or an image of me."

"How could you be the Sleepwalker?"

"I think," said Chantel, explaining and understanding at the same time, "that all I saw, felt and experienced was made up in my mind. I had to face myself, and I did. I faced my memories and my doubts and my fears."

"So how do you know that your parents are dead?"

"I guess . . . I guess I don't know. It's just one of my fears." Chantel felt much better. "Thank you, sister."

"I know how important it is to hope that your family is alive. I know how it feels like to be alone. Sometimes I think I am the only Winged One left."

"Maybe you aren't," said Chantel. "Owl told me that all the Winged Ones were dead, and then I met you. Maybe there are more Winged Ones that survived. Maybe we will find them on our quest."

"And maybe we will find your parents," added Laluna softly.

The sleeping gowns were fleecy and big. After a quick meal of sweet foods, Chantel and Laluna journeyed through the huge, icy building to their bedroom.

"Do you regret seeing the Sleepwalker—I mean, facing yourself?" Laluna asked.

Chantel shook her head. "It made me stronger. It made me realize what is important. How can I regret an experience that helped me know myself better?"

"I am glad you came out of it unharmed."

Chantel smiled, but as she remembered the vision of the strange death of the woman, the vision of Owl with Fawn in his beak, and the difficulty she had resisting Aquila's smooth tongue, she wondered if she had truly escaped unharmed. "I am sure to have nightmares tonight," she thought.

But no nightmares troubled her sleep. Instead she had a dream so strange and confusing that she couldn't remember it in the morning.

⚜

During breakfast, Laluna took out a piece of paper.

"You were talking in your sleep last night," Laluna said. "It was in a different language. I didn't understand it, but I wrote down what you said as best I could."

Laluna handed the paper to Chantel, who tried to read it.

Trapa raf dna tnereffid erew yeht ecno
Straeh ynam yb devol erew htob tub
Emit hguorht dnob a yb detcennoc
Enim eb lliw dna eno era yeht won

"I have no idea what this means," Chantel said.

"But I do."

Chantel heard a threatening voice in her head, a voice she had never heard before.

"The prophecy has started, and I am waiting for you. I don't know who you are yet, but I will find out soon."

"Did you hear that?" Chantel jumped up and looked around the big room.

"What?" said Laluna.

"What did you hear, Chantel?" Aurora asked anxiously.

"You didn't hear that terrible voice?" Chantel cried.

"Don't worry, my child," another voice—a kind, familiar one—filled her mind. It was Mother Nature. "It is just trying to scare you. It can't harm you."

"Who is it?"

"The Evil One. It knows that you exist now, but it does not know who you are or where you are. All it did was send out a message with the hope that you would hear it. The Evil One was lucky that you were listening. Aquila Bellum must have told it that you are in the mountains. Be careful from now on. The helpers of the Darkness are on the lookout."

"We have to hurry," Chantel said to Laluna and Aurora. "The Evil One knows about me!"

Laluna took the paper and put it in her pouch. She knew the message had to be important. They finished their breakfast and began to pack their belongings.

CHAPTER TWENTY-FIVE

The Golden Sword

"Follow me," Aurora said. "I spoke with the council, and because you have passed the Sleepwalker's test, it has decided to entrust you with our most valuable belonging."

Aurora led Chantel, Laluna and Fox to the main tower beside the entrance hall. They climbed up the staircase, but when they reached the top, they faced a blank wall. There was no door or passageway. Just as she was about to question Aurora, the ceiling above their heads opened up like the petals of a flower and the last step rose up like a flying sled. They entered the hidden hall of the ancient council.

Chantel looked around. She and her friends were in the middle of a room and surrounded by a huge, ring-shaped table. The council members sat on the other side of the table. Their eyes were fixed on something just above Chantel's head, and they were humming an ancient tune. It was the tune sung during the annual celebration of the Golden Sword.

Chantel looked up.

The Golden Sword hovered in the air above her head.

"Take it and protect it well. You hold the future of all of us in your hands. May our prayers and hopes protect you," said the council in one voice.

Chantel raised her arms and opened her hands. The Golden Sword started to sparkle and float downwards. Gently the hilt came to rest in her hands. She closed her fingers around it. It felt both light and heavy at the same time—light in her hands and heavy in her heart.

Then the Sword came alive. It glowed even more brightly and began to quiver. Chantel could feel two forces flowing into her fingertips—an evil power and a good power. And then she felt something else—something glorious. It was another power—a balancing power—that made her feel light enough to float. Magenta light, like that caused by the two moons coming together, started to surround Chantel.

The elders gasped. Indeed, Chantel would be able to wield the dark and light powers. No other human being had ever been able to call upon both powers, but if Chantel was not careful, she could be killed by either of them.

The engraved words on the blade started to blaze: "For Us to Share."

The elders stood up and applauded. In entrusting her with the Sword, they had given Chantel great responsibility. She knew it and accepted it with honor.

Before she lowered the Sword and placed it securely on her belt, Chantel turned slowly and looked into the eyes of each council member. "I will protect your most valuable possession with my life. I will bring us freedom and happiness again," she repeated over and over again before looking into Aurora's eyes.

"Follow me," Aurora said, snapping her fingers.

Instantly Chantel, Laluna, Fox and Aurora were standing in the ice garden. They walked quickly and silently past the sculpted flowers and trees, glancing at a gardener carving a new bush with bell-shaped ice berries. They moved through the castle gates and soon reached the entrance of the tunnel.

"Norfalk is expecting you on the other side," Aurora said. "Take good care of yourself, princess."

"You have not told me everything," Chantel said.

"What do you mean?" Aurora asked, bewildered.

"You did not tell me that Aquila Bellum killed his parents." Chantel was not sure if this was true or not, but she needed to find out.

"I didn't want to scare you too much," said Aurora. "But yes, you are right. He murdered at least part of his family. He set fire to their house while his parents and sister were sleeping inside. This was before we moved here. We found the bodies of his father and sister, but we did not find his mother."

"Do you know if he killed my parents, too?"

"I don't know," Aurora answered. She paused and looked into Chantel's eyes. "But I do believe that you are a child of the mountains. I can feel it. Your ancestors are from the mountains. The mountain's strength beats in your heart."

"Me, a mountain child?"

Chantel thought about the calm the mountains had always brought her and the feelings the smell of the edelweiss invoked.

"I am a mountain child," she whispered proudly.

"One more thing," Aurora said. She pulled out a piece

of material from under her cloak. It was another cloak, as soft and warm as fur, although it seemed to be sewn from snowflakes. A thin ribbon of material gathered the hood together. "You can tie your hood around your neck so it won't slip off during the night. It will hide your Golden Braid."

"Thank you," Chantel said, slipping off her old cloak and putting the new one on.

"And, of course, one for you, too, my dear," said Aurora, handing Laluna a similar cloak that had holes for her wings. Laluna beamed.

After kissing their cheeks, Aurora waved good-bye, and Chantel, Laluna and Fox set off into the tunnel.

CHAPTER TWENTY-SIX

Getting Ready

Mouse watched several huge wolverines and ugly hyenas pace around the snowy field below his hideout. A tall man was busy building something, but Mouse was too far away to see what it was. The man continued to build late into the night.

The morning after everything was quiet. Only a few black ravens circled high in the sky, screeching at an eagle that had swooped too close to their nests. The wolverines, hyenas and the tall man were gone. The field was a spotless white carpet. Although it hadn't snowed during the night, it appeared as if it had, since the field showed no sign of the previous day's activities.

"What happened last night?" Mouse wondered. He started to think. "Behind the snowfield is the Lake of Clouds. Chantel must have gone there to retrieve the Golden Sword. The tall man was building something." Then it clicked. "Perhaps he built a trap!"

Confident that he was right, Mouse was less sure of what to do.

"Wait," a voice within told him. "Get ready. You will know what to do when the time comes."

When they reached the end of the tunnel, Chantel, Laluna and Fox greeted Norfalk warmly.

"Welcome back," the huge gargoyle said with a smile, his stone teeth glinting in the sunlight. "How nice to see you again. I hope you found what you were looking for."

"Yes, I did. Thank you," Chantel said.

Laluna spoke quietly to Fox, who flew into the clouds and disappeared. A few minutes later he returned and landed on Laluna's shoulder.

"He didn't see anything suspicious out there," Laluna said.

"Let's go then," replied Chantel.

"Good luck," said Norfalk. "Be careful. The Snow Walker is out there, and he desperately wants what you have."

They walked up the hill through the clouds, clinging to each other tightly. They were glad when they emerged from the Lake of Clouds and saw the blue sky again. Although everything seemed calm and peaceful, Chantel's neck hairs stood on end and her braid was heavy. She gestured to Laluna, and they hid behind a large boulder.

"Something isn't right."

"I feel it, too," said Laluna.

"We have to be very careful. I think Aquila Bellum is close. He's probably waiting for us. But where?"

Chantel motioned for Laluna to use hand signs from then on. Then she peeked from behind the boulder to get her bearings. She pointed to a tall tree that stood fifty meters away, up the hill. They both ran to it at the same time, unaware of all the eyes that were following them.

Chantel pointed to the next tree, and they started to run for it. The snow was very deep, and they sank into it up to their knees. Their run was more a fight against the white mass of heavy snow. They didn't make much progress, and they started to sweat. Laluna stumbled and her whole body sank into the snow. She pulled herself up and tried to run again.

Then everything happened at once. The ground turned upside down. A big net catapulted upwards and caught Chantel and Laluna in its center. Chunks of snow and dirt flew into the air. When the snow settled, Chantel and Laluna were imprisoned in a web of thick ropes. They dangled in the midst of a pack of growling, hissing wolverines and hyenas. More fearsome than any of the beasts, Aquila Bellum faced the net with a sinister smile stretched across his red face.

"So we meet again, child," he jeered, "but you knew this would happen. It's foolish to take the same path twice, especially when someone is hunting you, but that is what all inexperienced mountain hikers do because they are afraid of getting lost. That's why they are so easy to track."

"Let us go!" cried Chantel, struggling against the ropes.

"HA!" Aquila laughed. "The net holds you tight, like a butterfly in a spiderweb. This time you cannot use your Magic Staff. Genius!" He laughed again. "You have something I want. It belongs to me. Give it to me now, and I will let you live. If not, my wolverines and the hyenas will have their fun with you, and then I will just pluck it . . ."

Suddenly a tall creature came flying down from the hill

and landed on Aquila Bellum, hitting Aquila's head with the blunt edge of a massive sword. Aquila toppled, unconscious, into the snow. The creature stood up and turned towards the wolverines and hyenas, brandishing his sword and his claws.

Chantel and Laluna clung to each other in the net as they watched the creature battle Aquila's beasts. The animals were strong and skilled fighters. As one group of beasts attacked, the other circled slowly around the strange armored creature. They snarled and hissed. Saliva dripped from their mouths and sizzled into the snow.

The Mighty Warrior moved deftly and swiftly. His sword sliced through the bodies of the attacking beasts with ease. Terrible howls filled the air.

Although one wolverine bit through his armor, the Mighty Warrior didn't show any pain. He grabbed the wolverine and broke its neck with his mighty paw. Soon the snow was drenched with blood. Then one hyena bit his sword-carrying arm, sinking its long teeth deep into his flesh, and dragged him down. The warrior's sword fell from his paw, but he used his knifelike claws to slice through the hyena's throat. Just as he pulled himself up, another wolverine leaped onto his back and tried to bite into his neck. The Mighty Warrior jumped up, turned in midair and landed heavily on his back, crushing the wolverine beneath him. He found his sword in the snow, grabbed it and, quickly recovering, sliced an attacking hyena in two. There were only two wolverines left, and they were barely able to stand. As the Mighty Warrior moved towards them, they turned around and slunk away into the mountains.

Covered in blood, the Mighty Warrior limped over to

Chantel and Laluna. He slashed his sword across the ropes, slicing the net apart, and Chantel and Laluna fell onto the snow beneath them.

He leaned down and helped them up. He did not see Aquila Bellum rising out of the snow, lifting his heavy sword into the air to deliver a deadly blow.

"Watch out!" cried Chantel, but it was too late.

Aquila's sword hit the Mighty Warrior on the side of his head. He tumbled and fell. A deep cut opened and blood poured onto the snow.

Chantel freed herself from the ropes and pulled out the Golden Sword. She lifted it over her head.

"Is this what you want?" she yelled at Aquila.

Aquila started to laugh.

"You wish to fight me?" he said, walking towards her, his red eyes glowing like flames. The sight of the Golden Sword made him wild. He could see the dark power pulsating in it, and he trembled with excitement. "Soon it will be mine," he thought.

"So be it," he cried. "I will try to make your death painless."

He lifted his sword and pounced. Chantel stood her ground, deflecting his first blow. The Golden Sword started to glow and sparkle. Chantel felt its power in her hands. It felt almost like the power in her Magic Staff, except the power of the Sword filled her body and gave her strength— more strength than she had ever known.

Moving the Golden Sword swiftly through the air, she forced Aquila to retreat, but he quickly found new footing. He brought his sword down fast and hard several times, but Chantel blocked his heavy blows. After a few more blows were exchanged, Chantel stumbled backward and tripped over a rock. She tried to scramble back to her feet. Aquila stood over her with the tip of his blade pointed at her chest. Lying on her back, she clung to the Golden Sword, but Aquila pinned it with his foot. Her mind raced as Aquila prepared to plunge his sword into her, his eyes filled with hatred.

Suddenly everything became calm. The Golden Sword began to hum. Aquila froze, as if the humming had cast a spell over him.

His face began to change. His wild beard disappeared. His eyes turned from red to blue. His hair grew longer and softer, and a silver band ringed his head, dropping to a point in the middle of his brow. A small claw hung from its tip like a jewel.

His brutal, weathered face had changed into the face of a kind woman.

Chantel, bewildered by the transformation, stared into the woman's eyes.

"How is this possible?" Chantel had seen this face before. She had seen it in her bathroom mirror in her castle. The face looked like her own, only older.

"Find me," Chantel heard a female voice say in her mind while the lips on the face in front of her moved, "but do not search for a human."

"Mother?" Chantel whispered.

Aquila held his sword even higher over his head, preparing to deliver the final blow. But he hesitated.

He saw a reflection in Chantel's eyes, but it was not his. His eyes widened in recognition and shock. "It . . . it can't be!" he whispered.

His face began to change back to its hairy, dirty self. The sweet blue eyes melted away, replaced by red angry ones.

Chantel acted quickly. She pulled the Golden Sword out from under Aquila's foot and pointed it at Aquila's chest. She thought about a white light, as white as Aurora's snowflake dress. The power in the Golden Sword pulsated, and a radiant light erupted from the tip of it, hitting Aquila in the chest. It lifted him up high into the air, and he landed hard in the snow far away.

Chantel did not move for a while. She just lay there thinking about what had just happened. After a few long moments, she got up slowly, leaning on the Golden Sword. She could see where Aquila had landed, but she didn't know if he was dead or not.

"You released the light power of the Golden Sword," she heard Mother Nature's voice in her head. "Well done, Chantel. You channeled your emotions, and you weren't tempted by the dark power."

Laluna ran to Chantel and gave her a big hug. "You're alive!" she cried.

"But is he?" cried Chantel, gesturing to the creature that had just saved their lives. The Mighty Warrior lay still in the snow, surrounded by dead hyenas and wolverines. His fur was matted with blood. Chantel and Laluna bent over his body. A groan escaped from his lips.

"Who are you?" Chantel asked. "Why did you help us?"

The Mighty Warrior slowly opened his eyes and looked at Chantel. "Don't you recognize me?" he whispered.

Chantel looked deep into his green eyes. There was something very familiar about them.

"Mouse?" she whispered. "Mouse! What happened? How can it be?"

"I will explain everything later, but now we must go. We are not safe here."

Laluna kneeled down and quickly cleaned the open wound above the Mighty Warrior's eye with cloths from her pack, and then wrapped a bandage around his head. When she was done, she helped him up.

"Where is the Snow Walker?" Mouse asked.

"He is . . ." Chantel turned to point to the spot where Aquila Bellum had fallen and gasped. Aquila was gone. A trail of footprints and blood led into the forest.

"He must be gathering more beasts," said the Mighty Warrior. "We must hurry."

Chantel and Laluna collected their scattered supplies. Chantel secured the Golden Sword to her belt. They moved as quickly as possible up the ridge. Chantel gazed back once for a final look at the mountains and the Lake of Clouds. The sun was going to rest; her orange and red rays painted the mountains in a warm, mysterious light.

"How peaceful and pretty it looks," Chantel thought. "If only it really were so."

⚋⚋

As they reached the mountain cliffs, the Mighty Warrior changed back into Mouse.

"Amazing," said Laluna.

"What happened to you after I fell into the tunnel beside the Endless Gorge?" asked Chantel.

"I managed to get across the Gorge, and Fin helped me learn how to use and control my gift."

"Changing into the Mighty Warrior, you mean?"

"Yes." Mouse smiled proudly.

"I'm glad we're together again," Chantel said. "I missed you a lot."

"I won't leave you again," Mouse said. "I promise."

They found a small cave where they could spend the night. After a quick meal of worms Mouse had collected and a bit of the bread and cheese Aurora had sent with them, Laluna and Chantel, bundled in blankets, fell fast asleep.

Mouse stayed awake for a while. He listened to Chantel and Laluna's quiet, rhythmic breathing and thought about the day's events.

"Well done, Mouse. I'm glad I chose you to protect Chantel."

Mouse smiled. He knew that voice very well. "Stay vigilant," Mother Nature warned. "There are more battles to fight."

It was dark outside the cave, except for a few shimmering silvery blue moonbeams. The sound of a mountain horn bellowed and echoed across the mountains, and Mouse could hear the shrieking and screaming of the mountain creatures. He was not too concerned because the sounds were very faint, but he knew the wild beasts were coming after them. The blood-red moon slowly appeared behind the shifting clouds and grew very large.

Finally the events of the day caught up with Mouse and he fell asleep . . . with one eye open.

CHAPTER TWENTY-SEVEN

The Solenodon

Every creature has the right to exist—all the flowers, trees, birds, bees, wolves and wolverines, and every human. The One who wields both powers has the responsibility to decide what is right and what is wrong and act accordingly so that everything that exists does so in harmony.

From The Book of Erebus

Chantel awoke well rested, but she could still feel the bruises from the battle with Aquila the day before. Her left arm hurt, and her right hand was swollen and purple. Mouse was gone. "Probably gathering breakfast," she thought.

Just then Mouse peeked around the corner of the cave's entrance.

"All's clear," he said. "It's a fine, fresh morning. We have a long way to go before we reach Fin's place. Let's go. We can eat on the run."

"How are your injuries?" Chantel asked.

"The Mighty Warrior heals quickly," he said. Sure enough, his scars were almost gone. Only a thin red line was left from the vast cut that had crossed the side of his head.

Chantel gently shook Laluna awake. Laluna stretched and straightened out her wings. As she crawled out of the cave to join Fox for a morning flight, Chantel collected and packed all their belongings.

When Laluna and Fox returned, they all set off towards the valley, chomping on tree bark and a few berries. The cold and snow had left little to eat. By nightfall, they reached Fin's waterfall, their stomachs growling.

Everything was peaceful and quiet—too peaceful and too quiet. There were no birds singing their love songs and no squirrels chasing each other up and down the trees. And where were the Kowalis? Chantel's neck started to tingle, and she could feel the tug of her Golden Braid as it grew heavy.

It was cold and dark inside Fin's cave. No one was home.

"He must have gone to the castle as he had planned," Chantel said.

Laluna began to start a fire while Chantel went upstairs, spending a moment deeply inhaling the pungent edelweiss and thinking about Aurora's words and her mother's face. She looked out the window.

"Where *are* the Kowalis?" Chantel thought again.

BOOM!

Laluna ran upstairs. "What was that?"

"I don't know," said Chantel.

BOOM!

This time they recognized the sound. It was a drumbeat. Chantel's neck hair stood up straight.

"We have to get out of here," she said. "It's a trap."

They hurried downstairs, grabbed their belongings and ran towards the cave exit. Mouse jumped in front of them.

"Stop," he whispered, loud enough so just the girls could hear him. "They may be outside already. We can't go out there . . ."

The drumbeat became louder and more insistent. Heavy footsteps joined the beat and shook the ground.

"There must be hundreds of them," whispered Chantel.

Laluna ran back upstairs with Fox and pointed to the window. "Fly, my friend, and be our eyes," she said. "Find out what's happening, but don't get caught."

Fox crawled through the hidden window and jumped off its ledge. The wind was in his favor and carried him silently into the sky above the mountain plateau. Many fires flickered on the distant mountainside. The fires belonged to an army of evil beings, including the most dangerous creature of the mountain. No power could defeat that monster. Fox trembled as he quickly flew back to the waterfall.

Using his keen sense of smell and sound, he found the hidden window and climbed in. Laluna closed it and listened as Fox gave her the terrible news.

"There is an army of evil ones camped nearby," Laluna told Chantel and Mouse. "They have the Bush Dog Smellers with them. Those creatures can follow tracks that are weeks old. Soon they will find us. And there's something else out there, too—a creature so horrible that Fox can't even describe it."

Chantel looked around the cave. She tried to stay calm and focused. "There must be another way out. Fin would have thought of that." She took out her Magic Staff and concentrated. The power welled up in her body and spilled into the Staff. Its crystal turned green. Chantel moved in a circle, holding the Magic Staff away from her, pointing it in all directions. The green light shone on the bed where she had slept and on the kitchen table and bookshelves. When it hit the fireplace the light changed, becoming a deeper green.

"There, behind the fireplace," Chantel said. "The wall is very thin. Follow me."

Standing in front of the fireplace, she focused, sending more energy into the Magic Staff. She could feel its power grow. The crystal turned brighter, and Chantel started to breathe heavily. The power tried to overwhelm her again, but she stood her ground.

Slowly, a door in the wall behind the fireplace opened. Chantel let go of the power, and the crystal stopped glowing. She was perspiring, but she still felt strong.

Outside the drumbeats grew louder.

"Go through the door," Chantel commanded. "I will be right behind you."

Laluna and Mouse walked through the door and entered a tunnel. Fox followed right behind them.

Chantel went into the kitchen to look for rosemary. "Rosemary is used to relax muscles, but when taken in large doses, it causes irritation of the intestine and cramps and can immobilize any enemy," she remembered.

She found a basket full of the herb and dumped the dried branches all over the floor. Then she quickly followed her friends into the tunnel. The secret door closed behind her, becoming invisible again.

"Where does the tunnel go?" Mouse asked.

"I don't know," Chantel said, "but it's the only way out."

Mouse took the lead. After what seemed like a very long time, he exclaimed, "The Endless Gorge! We're at the Endless Gorge!"

They climbed out of the tunnel and stood on a small ledge. A few rocks slipped off it and fell into the abyss.

"What will you do?" said Laluna, turning to Chantel. "Fox and I can fly across, and Mouse is small enough for me to carry, but I can't carry you."

"I don't know, but I feel that help is coming. I sense a friend."

Then a familiar voice came from the misty darkness. "Chantel! I heard the drums and wondered if I would meet someone here."

It was the Rock Climber. "I smelled you and your friends. I'm glad you escaped," he said. "Climb into my hand and I will take you to the other side."

Laluna and Fox jumped off the ledge, opened their wings and flew into the air. The Rock Climber whistled, and the cliffs became alive.

Several hundred Rock Climbers came together and started to build a bridge by locking their arms and legs together. They started simultaneously on both sides of the Gorge. Both ends of the bridge grew quickly and they each formed half an arch. Before the ends reached each other, three Rock Climbers on either side ran up the arches and jumped into the air, catching each other and connecting to complete the bridge.

"Amazing," said Fox to himself, watching the bridge form from below.

Chantel's Rock Climber, carrying Chantel, started to run across the backs of his brothers and sisters. Moments later he set Chantel down on the other side of the Gorge.

"Thank you!" said Chantel.

"Any time, Princess of Freedom," replied the Rock Climber.

⁓✦⁓

"In there!" cried Aquila Bellum. A big, open gash crossed his forehead. Dried blood flaked from his skin, and he walked with a limp.

His Bush Dog Smellers sniffed the zigzagging tracks that led them through the waterfall and into Fin's cave. They destroyed the cave in seconds. They bit books in two and tossed them across the floor. They smashed the kitchen table and tore apart Fin's rocking chair. The Bush Dogs sniffed and sniffed, inhaling the rosemary. They turned in circles, unable to find any tracks.

Soon the Bush Dogs started to have cramps. Their intestines made terrible sounds, and their stomachs swelled. They howled in pain.

Aquila Bellum had lost Chantel again. He ran out of the cave and started to scream. But the hunt was not over yet. He blew into his mountain horn as hard as he could. After a few moments he blew again and waited for a reply. He didn't have to wait long.

A blood-curdling screech filled the air. His wolverines whimpered, backing away and tucking their tails between their legs, as the monster Fox had seen and been unable to describe swooped down from the sky.

A gush of wind blew loose earth into the air as a hairless creature with reddish-brown skin and a snout the size of a small tree stump landed on the mountain plateau.

It was a Solenodon, the deadliest hunter of the mountains. Its sharp claws tore at the ground, and its long tail, shaped like a lightning bolt, thrashed around its head. Its eyes were red like Aquila's, and its long teeth reflected the orange light of the evening sun.

"Come, my friend," Aquila Bellum hissed. "Fly and get that Golden Braid for me. Do not disappoint me."

The Solenodon lifted up into the air and shrieked. The sound was so horrible that even Aquila tensed. Then he laughed. No one could defeat the Solenodon.

"Fly, my cursed one. Get that girl for me, dead or alive."

CHAPTER TWENTY-EIGHT

A Terrible Evening

"In a day, we will reach the main waterfall," said Mouse. "From there, it's only a two-day hike home. Let's find a good resting spot for the night."

"A tree, as usual?" Chantel said, smiling.

"Of course," Mouse replied. He felt very good about himself and it showed. Full of energy, he ran off to find the right tree.

Chantel took Laluna's hand. "I'm glad that we found each other. I always felt so lonely. I know I have Owl, but he's more like a guardian. You'll meet him soon. He can be solemn and protective, but he means well."

"I can't wait," replied Laluna. "I want to ask him about the Winged Ones, and if he knows of any owl that is tiny with ghost-white feathers. If the owl of my village still lives, perhaps other Winged Ones do, too."

The evening was warm, and the air smelled fresh, like it did after a long summer rainfall. Chantel and Laluna walked side by side for a while, discussing Mouse and his ability to change.

"Where *is* Mouse?" Chantel asked.

"This way, I think," said Laluna, running ahead, passing through a forest of small trees and into a green clearing.

When Chantel reached the clearing, Laluna stood in the center of it, her sword drawn.

"Stay away!" Laluna yelled. "Go back into the forest."

Fox circled Laluna in a frantic flight.

Chantel's neck started to tingle. She looked around but could not see anything dangerous. Then a massive shadow appeared on the ground. Chantel looked up. A creature, its outlines coal-black against the fiery-red evening sky, raced down towards the clearing, a blur of leathery wings, red eyes and long, sharp claws. The creature was heading straight for her! With a great and sudden jerk, the Solenodon veered to the left, so close to Chantel's head that she could smell its foul breath. With its claws raised, it dove towards Laluna. Laluna screamed as the Solenodon crashed on top of her with a great thump.

Her scream stopped abruptly. The creature's claws wrapped around Laluna's lifeless body, and it started to pick at her wing with its ugly beak. Fox tried to distract the monster by landing on its head and trying to slice him with his own sharp wingtips, but the monster did not even notice him.

"NO!" screamed Chantel, racing towards the beast with the Golden Sword raised in one hand and the Magic Staff in the other.

But the Solenodon was quick. It sprung into the air with a single flap of its massive wings. Laluna dangled from its claws.

"NO!" Chantel cried again. "Laluna! Come back!"

The Mighty Warrior crashed out of the forest. Mouse

had heard the yelling and had transformed quickly, but he was too late. He looked on helplessly as the creature carried Laluna away.

Chantel gripped her Magic Staff while a strange feeling swallowed her heart. It was as strong as her love for Laluna, but as opposite to it as light is to darkness.

It was hatred.

Tears streamed down her cheeks. "Laluna!" she cried. But her shouts were useless. The monster flew higher and higher. She felt a power swirl within her, cold and relentless, fueled by her hatred. Hate against that monster, the Darkness and Aquila Bellum.

The power grew very strong very quickly. Shaking so violently that she could barely stand, she raised her Staff and pointed the crystal towards the Solenodon.

The pulse of power turned to a ripping force that threatened to tear her in two. She screamed. The power was killing her. And then she had a vision:

She saw a tall man dressed in yellow. He stood beside a simple tent in a sea of sand and raised his left arm, pointing his finger upwards. A red light came out of his finger, illuminating a single cloud in the blue sky.

"Look at me, my princess," he said. "It is time. Do not be afraid. Do not be overwhelmed by this hatred. Remember love and follow your heart. Your heart will lead you to me. Soon we will meet, and I will explain everything to you. The power is within you, princess. You have the strength to use it—just don't forget love."

"Love?" Chantel thought. "All I feel right now is hatred."

The Staff shook in her hands as the power flew through

her arm and into it. Suddenly a red light exploded from the crystal, zigzagging into the sky. It hit the Solenodon directly in the chest. The beast screamed in pain as its skin flashed red, then orange, and then violet.

BOOM!

The Solenodon exploded.

~₩~

The earth trembled and shock waves raced across the land towards the West. As the waves reached the far island, the second glass chain that held the Evil One broke. She smiled in the darkness of her cave.

"Soon," she thought. "Soon I will be able to return to the lands and finish what I started so long ago. Two chains have been broken. Only one is left. After the first one was broken I was able to release the first red lightning bolt to destroy the village of the Winged Ones. Now I have another lightning bolt available. But I must be patient. I must use it when the time is right."

~₩~

Eronimus Finsh was strolling along the castle's garden for his usual evening walk. The air was warm and he was at peace with himself. As he looked towards the mountains, he saw the blood-red moon hovering above the snow-covered peaks.

"The dark-red moon is out early tonight," he remarked. "A bad omen."

Just as the words had left his mouth, he saw the red light and the explosion. "The red lightning bolt of the Darkness," he thought. "The Snow Walker has the Golden Sword! Chantel has been defeated!"

He concentrated and used his powers to hover up into the air until he could see far into the distance and make out the speck holding the Staff.

"It isn't the Snow Walker—it's Chantel! She's holding the Staff and the Sword! She unleashed the red lightning bolt! Chantel!" he shouted. "What have you done?"

Fin felt the Darkness rise in his body, and it started to tear at his mind.

"All of us have a dark side, but we must not be overwhelmed by it. Hope and love will always bring us back to our true path," Fin whispered to himself. "'For Us to Share.'"

Just as Fin's mind cleared, Owl flew up into the sky. "What happened?" Owl asked Fin. "I heard an explosion."

"Chantel somehow used the ancient power of the Darkness," replied Fin. "She released the red lightning bolt."

Owl's feathers turned a shade grayer as he remembered the day a similar blot destroyed his people, the Winged Ones. He gulped, thinking of his own actions that dreadful day, his own *inactions*, and his secret tie to the Evil One.

"All of us have a dark side, but we must not be overwhelmed by it. Hope and love will always bring us back to our true path," Owl muttered under his breath.

Owl and Fin shook in midair as they both battled their dark sides.

"Laluna!" Chantel screamed.

Laluna's lifeless body tumbled down to earth, dropping out of the sky like a rock. The colors of her wings were dull and dark.

"I've got her," the Mighty Warrior yelled. He jumped up as high as he could and caught Laluna. He landed softly in the grass, cradling her in his arms. Laluna did not stir. Her clothing was ripped and blood was running down her face. One of her wings was badly torn.

"Is she . . ." Chantel couldn't say the word. She looked at Mouse, tears running down her cheeks. "She can't be. Tell me . . . please tell me . . ."

Another voice answered Chantel's plea.

"You did it. You used the dark power."

"Go away! Leave me alone!"

Chantel covered her ears, but the dreadful voice in her mind continued, "Didn't it feel good to use the red lightning bolt? Wasn't it exhilarating? Can you feel the dark power uniting us? I can sense you now. I can feel your suffering. I can feel your hate for me, but I don't mind. Your hate only binds our minds closer together."

Chantel looked at Mouse and at Laluna's limp body. The Mighty Warrior rested his ear on Laluna's chest. Chantel was alone with the voice of the Evil One.

"Your Soul Mate helped you. I tried to keep you two apart. I try to keep all Soul Mates apart. It makes everyone weaker and easier to manipulate. Your emotions must have been very strong for your Soul Mate to find you."

Chantel held her throbbing head. "Leave me alone!" she cried.

"Yes, I will leave you now. Soon we will meet in person, but before then I warn you: look after your loved ones."

CHAPTER TWENTY-NINE

Saving Laluna

"She is still breathing, but her breath is shallow and weak," the Mighty Warrior said.

The voice in Chantel's head was gone. Dazed, she looked at the Mighty Warrior.

"Mother Nature is her only hope," continued the Mighty Warrior. "Jump on my back, Chantel, and hold on."

Chantel wrapped her arms around his neck and squeezed her knees into his sides the way she used to when riding on Owl's back in the castle courtyard when she was younger.

The Mighty Warrior lunged forward and was off like the wind. His strong, long legs carried them quickly over the countryside. Fox flew in front of them, leading the way.

"We need you, Mother Nature. Where are you?" Chantel cried in her mind.

"I'm here, Chantel," she heard Mother Nature's voice. "Fox knows where to go. I will be waiting for you."

"Run quickly, Mouse," said Chantel. "Follow Fox. Mother Nature is waiting for us."

Seconds turned into minutes, and minutes turned into hours. The silvery-blue moon, high up in the sky, tried its best to provide enough light so that Mouse could find his way.

⁓✦⁓

The sun had just started to show her brilliant rays when the Mighty Warrior reached the waterfall. With his last bit of strength, he lay Laluna on the soft moss near the river's edge. Chantel slid off his back and curled up in the moss next to Laluna. The Mighty Warrior sat down and changed back into Mouse. Dizzy and sick to his stomach, he lay back on the soft moss and passed out, nestled in the crook of Chantel's arm.

Chantel watched over Laluna until she heard the crackling sound of dried leaves. She turned to face Mother Nature. No crystals glimmered from her ears. No dewdrops hung in her hair. Her skin was gray like a sky that hasn't seen sun for weeks.

"Your senses are very good," Mother Nature said. She sounded tired.

"Can you help her? Can you save Laluna?" asked Chantel.

"Go back to sleep. You need your rest. Do not worry, my Princess of Freedom. I will look after Laluna."

Chantel turned on her side and immediately fell back asleep in the moss cushions. But it was not a peaceful sleep. Red eyes and red lightning bolts and the awful voice of the Evil One haunted her dreams.

"You have felt the power of the Darkness. You also know now how it feels to hate. Soon you will be mine," the Evil One whispered. "You released me from my second bond, and soon the third one—the final one—will fall, too. It is only a matter of time."

∘⌐┅┅┅⌐∘

Mother Nature carried Laluna deep underground. She waded through swampy tunnels, slid down passages of moss and murmured the secret words to open the seven gates of roots until she reached a warm cave filled with the smell of lavender and roses. Many small and large animals lived in the huge cave. Some were limping, while others lay quietly on moss beds with bandages on their arms, legs or heads. Hundreds of crystals covered the ceiling, reflecting the lights of many burning candles on rock shelves.

Mother Nature washed Laluna's wounds and covered them with a special healing ointment. She put green leaves from a willow tree on them to protect the wounds from dirt and disease. She dripped warm tea on Laluna's cracked lips and placed her on a bed of the softest green moss beside a small creek that ran through the cave.

Then she lit a violet candle and set it on a stone near Laluna. The candlelight flickered and smoked. Its fumes were soothing and calming. Laluna's breathing, however, was still weak. Mother Nature took deep breaths as she prepared to call on the healing strength of nature. It was Laluna's last hope.

CHAPTER THIRTY

The
Journey Home

One starts many adventures and tries many different things without knowing what the outcomes will be. Most stop too soon, fearful of failure, but if one is not willing to fail, one will never achieve success. So be strong and follow your instincts, Last Descendant, even though you might fail.

From The Book of Erebus

When the sun peeked over the mountains, Chantel and Mouse woke up. Both were stiff and weak and had pounding headaches.

"What do we do now?" asked Chantel.

"Continue to the castle," said Mouse. "We should be

there in two days if we don't encounter any problems, but after last night's events everybody will know where we are."

"What do you mean?"

"The red light and the explosion of the winged monster. How did you do that? I have never seen so much power before in my life. You stood there, almost in a trance, and you looked so angry and so intense that even I was scared."

"It was hatred," whispered Chantel. "It felt awful. I hope I never feel it again."

"You must learn how to control it," said Mouse.

"How can I learn if nobody knows about the lost colors?"

"You will find a way, one day."

As they packed their belongings and set off once again on their journey home, Chantel whispered, "There was something else, too. I had a vision."

"A vision?"

"Yes. A tall man came and spoke to me. Without him, the power of the Darkness would have overwhelmed me. He reminded me of love while I was consumed with hate."

"Who was he?" Mouse asked.

"I don't know," Chantel said. Had the Evil One told her the truth? Was the man really her Soul Mate? Why should she trust the Evil One? "The man used the code words and was surrounded by golden sand," Chantel continued.

"The only place I know where there is golden sand is in the land of the South," said Mouse. "It's not a very friendly place, but maybe that's where we must go next."

The day passed without any complications. Mouse located a wonderful tree with big branches to sleep on. Chantel selected a wide one, and Fox came flying down to lie beside her. As usual, Mouse chose a branch near the top of the tree.

The night was cold, quiet and dark. Clouds as black as the night sky surrounded the two moons, and a bitter breeze signaled the end of the warm days in the valley. Autumn was knocking on the door. Chantel sensed the change in the air.

"The green will be gone soon," she thought. She smiled. "But the leaves will change to yellow and then to red. The hills that lead to the mountains will look so pretty—as pretty and as colorful as Laluna's wings."

Chantel listened to the wind and thought about Laluna. Thinking about family reminded her of the moment when Aquila's face had turned into her mother's. Had she been hallucinating? Would she really find her mother?

Finally she fell asleep, and the moons appeared from behind the clouds to watch over their princess.

CHAPTER THIRTY-ONE

Friends

Chantel opened her eyes, disturbed by noises beneath the tree.

"Mouse?"

He was gone.

She looked down from her branch and pulled out her sword and Magic Staff. Two wolves were pacing around the trunk. One was black with shiny yellow eyes. The other one was gray with crystal blue eyes. They were not snarling or red-eyed like Aquila's beasts. The black one noticed the leaves rustle. He stopped, and the gray one did, too. And then they did the most extraordinary thing: They crouched forward and lowered their snouts until their noses touched the ground. They were bowing.

They raised their heads.

"Don't worry," said the black wolf to Chantel. "We're not here to hurt you. It is time that we came to help you. Our pack lives on the other side of the mountains, close to the ocean, in a forest where the land of the North meets the land of the West. When we heard the explosion and saw the red lightning bolt last night, we had to see for ourselves what had happened. We despise the Darkness. It has brought us nothing but death and misery."

Chantel climbed down the tree. Fox flew at a safe distance above them.

"We are honored to meet you, Princess of Freedom." The wolves bowed their heads again in respect. Then they looked her straight in the eyes.

"You don't have to worry about what lies behind you. We will protect you. Mouse already went ahead to scout out what lies ahead of you."

"Thank you," Chantel said. "What are your names?"

"I am Thidrek," said the black wolf.

"And my name is Orkaden," said the gray wolf.

"You will find Mouse up that path," said Thidrek. "Good luck on your journey, princess. May the moons always guide you."

"Will I see you again?" asked Chantel.

"We will be there when you need us," Orkaden replied, "and when you do, the Winged Ones will be ready, too. Our pack is still strong and always ready to fight the evil ones."

"Winged Ones!" Chantel exclaimed. "What Winged Ones? I thought they had all been killed by the red lightning bolt."

"Not all are dead. Some survived, and they have been living with us ever since. Three of the four Young Ones who will form the circle of light are alive. The fourth one is believed to be alive, too, and they are looking for her."

"Her?"

"Yes," Orkaden replied. "She is the missing link. The one who will complete the circle. It is said that the four Young

Ones together will help stop the Evil One from returning to the four lands."

"Do you know her name?" Chantel asked.

"They call her Laluna. But we must leave now. The evil beings still seek you. We will distract them. Hurry! Mouse is waiting for you up the hill behind the gray bush."

The wolves turned and ran towards the main waterfall.

"Laluna!" Chantel grabbed her belongings and ran up the hill. Fox flew in front of her, leading the way. "If only I could let Laluna know that she is not alone, that she is special and important!"

When they reached the top, Fox landed on Chantel's shoulder.

"Slowly now, and quietly," Fox whispered into Chantel's ear. "Hide behind the bush over there, beside the old rock, and don't move. We're getting closer to the castle. Mouse told me to show you the way."

Chantel had never heard Fox's voice before. Unlike the hissing voice of the Vampire Bat Brutus, Fox's voice was soft and gentle, like a whispered lullaby.

Chantel followed Fox's instructions. She waited for a few more minutes.

"Over here." Chantel heard Mouse but could not see him. "To your left, ten meters down."

Chantel looked around and saw Mouse's tail twitching under a red bush. She moved quietly and quickly.

"Look over there," Mouse said. "On that misty hill stands your castle. Nobody can see it. And nobody must see us from now on or the castle will be in jeopardy."

"I have an idea," Chantel said. "Come close to me. I

will use the Staff's magic to make us invisible." Chantel repeated Fin's words in her mind: "Water: Swimming in invisibility? You will rise again. If you think blue, you will become invisible." Then she whispered, "Mouse, jump into my pocket, and, Fox, sit on my shoulder."

Chantel thought about the color blue. She visualized lakes and blue eyes and sweet blueberries, and she called upon enough power to become invisible. Chantel stood up from behind the red bush.

She walked briskly down the hill towards the plateau. As she walked through the mist, she saw her castle appear slowly and she let go of the power.

"Home!" Chantel thought as she, Mouse and Fox became visible once again.

CHAPTER THIRTY-TWO

Home,
But Not Safe

Chantel dropped to her knees from exhaustion. That was the longest she'd ever held on to the Staff's power. Mouse jumped out of her pocket. When she had regained enough strength to stand up, they all moved towards the castle gates. As they passed through, Chantel noticed that the sword forged into the iron had a light shine to it. When they reached the castle doors, they did not have to knock. Owl swung the doors open and spread his big wings to hug Chantel.

"Welcome back, Chantel," Owl said, with tears in his eyes. "Come in, my dear. We've been waiting for you."

His feathers tickled her face, and she felt the familiar feeling of protection and love. She had made it. She was back home.

Chantel, Fox and Mouse entered the big hall and followed Owl into the kitchen, where Fin sat at the table enjoying a cup of warm tea and a pipe. The odor of his favorite tobacco filled the kitchen.

Fox landed on Chantel's shoulder and whispered, "Trouble."

Indeed, Chantel's neck tingled. But she was home, safe. What could harm her here? She looked around the kitchen. There were fresh flowers on the table in a silver vase, and soup bubbled in a pot over the fire.

She looked into Fin's eyes and sensed where the feeling of danger was coming from. He looked different. With a grim look on his face, Fin stood up and walked over to Chantel. He left his lit pipe on the table.

"How are you doing, princess?" he asked. His smile was insincere.

Chantel took a step back. "I'm fine, although I'm worried about Laluna."

"Are you sure you're fine?"

"What do you mean?"

"I saw the red lightning bolt of the Darkness. I felt the energy that went through your body, and I felt the hatred in your heart." As he spoke his voice became louder. Then his face turned red, as red as a lightning bolt itself. "You have summoned the dark power of the ancient ones. How did you do it? How did you know?" His voice had turned into a scream.

"Calm down, Fin!" said Chantel, grasping the handle of her Staff and the hilt of the Golden Sword under her cloak and gripping them tightly.

"Don't patronize me, child," Fin yelled, his eyes filled with jealousy. "I have to know about the power."

Fin jumped towards Chantel's throat with his small herb knife open and raised. Chantel pulled the Golden Sword out of its sheath and held it in front of her. Frightened by the Sword, he tumbled backward, landing on the ground. His knife fell out of his hand and slid across the floor. The sunlight that came through the kitchen window reflected off the Golden Sword's blade and right into Fin's eyes, blinding him. He covered his face and started to moan. He tried to crawl under the table, but the Mighty Warrior blocked his way.

"I am sorry. Forgive me, Chantel," Fin cried. "The Darkness filled my mind. I don't know what happened."

"Have you shown the Evil One where the castle is?" Chantel demanded.

"No, I haven't," Fin whispered.

"Tell us the truth," the Mighty Warrior yelled as he picked Fin up from the ground with one paw.

"You are a Wise One," Chantel said. "You are part of the council of the lands. Your duty is to guide the people of the land and to be strong. You can't be overcome by your dark side."

Fin started to cry. "I have tried to find the secret of the power for many moon crossings. I have traveled all four lands extensively. I've read all the books and all the manuscripts I could find. I gave up my life to search and study so I would be ready for the day when the Last Descendant would come and require my help, so that I could teach all there is to know about the power of the relics and the Magic Staff. Then you come and found the powers right away. I've wasted my life. My whole life."

"You didn't waste your life. Reflect on what you know. You have taught me. You healed my wounds after the fight with the Vampire Bats. Without you, I would have never found the Sword, been able to use the Staff or defeat the

Bush Dog Smellers. You helped Mouse with your wisdom and understanding so he could find his way, too. You gave us all strength and knowledge so we could believe in ourselves. We all have to accept who we are. So get up and be the Wise One you are supposed to be."

Owl, Mouse, Fin and Fox looked at Chantel in awe. Everyone felt the power of her words. Everyone could see and feel her strength and determination.

"I'm sorry," repeated Fin, wiping the tears out of his eyes. "I don't know what came over me."

"These are trying times," said Owl. "We all have to be strong. Let's have something to eat. I prepared your favorite meal, Fin: fresh potato and spring onion soup. Come."

Owl flew to the fireplace. He thought about Chantel's words and how true they were, even for him. He also had to fight his dark side. He was sure that he would never harm Chantel; he loved her too much. But he had to find peace within himself and forgive himself for not helping his people.

⁓✷⁓

As they ate, Chantel looked at Fin.

"The Darkness got to him," Fox whispered into Chantel's ear. "He will never be the same again. I hope he will not betray us."

"What can we do?"

"I don't know, Chantel," Fox said.

Chantel looked at her Magic Staff.

Chantel remembered Fin's words: "Earth, represented by the color green. Earth: Hemmed in by steep walls? There is a ladder. If you think green, doors will open and walls will move." She whispered, "I wonder if green can close doors, not just open them. Can I close Fin's mind to the outside world using the Staff, so that he can't communicate with the evil beings?"

"Try it," Fox replied.

Chantel thought about green very carefully. She had to be soft and gentle with the power; otherwise she might destroy Fin's mind. She thought about the soft green moss near Mother Nature's waterfall and the gentle green of Fawn's eyes. As she visualized and closed the doors to Fin's mind, Fin did not notice anything, but someone else noticed the sudden change.

⚘

The Evil One, far away in her cave, felt the closing of Fin's mind. She had lost contact with him. She did not know it was Fin, for it was only a day ago that she had felt his turn to the Darkness. She hadn't had time to properly contact him. Now it was too late. She knew, however, that he was an important one, a Wise One. She smiled. Any person overcome by the Darkness was weakened forever, and a weak Wise One was a good sign. The Darkness was spreading.

"Aquila Bellum," she said in her mind, "listen."

"Yes, Evil One," Aquila responded. "I hear you."

"One of the Wise Ones was touched by the Darkness, but I lost contact with him. Be aware that we are getting stronger, and I will return soon," she said.

"Yes, Evil One."

"Do I sense a change in your feelings?" the Evil One suddenly asked.

"What do you mean?"

"You were touched by the light power. Has it weakened your commitment to me?"

"No. Of course not! I am committed to you, now and forever. I've just learned that I have to be more careful. I underestimated the strength of the Princess of Freedom."

"Princess of Freedom?"

"That is what they are calling the Last Descendant. But I will defeat her. I will make you proud of me. I will get you the four relics and the Golden Braid."

"Princess of Freedom," the Evil One mused. "Cute."

CHAPTER THIRTY-THREE

Asking for Help

Laluna's forehead was covered with sweat. The wounds inflicted by the Solenodon were infected and swollen. Mother Nature held her hand. Although she had summoned the entire healing power of nature, Laluna's fever was the same. The candlelight in the cave flickered violently. Mother Nature was getting weaker herself. She knew she was losing the battle against the poison in Laluna's blood, and she was not sure how much longer she could keep Laluna alive.

"I need help," she thought.

She got up and walked deeper into her cave until she reached a black lake. Black crystals covered the top of the cave, and the surface of the water looked like a huge mirror. She lit a single candle on an oval-shaped stone at the water's edge. The black crystals reflected the light, and the lake shimmered with hundreds of stars. Mother Nature stared into the water and spoke clearly and loudly.

"Listen to me, spirits of the lands, I need your help. Please come to me and give me strength." She closed her eyes and started to hum. It was the tune sung during the winter nights when all four spirits came together on top of the highest mountain to overlook the four lands, before everything had changed.

The flame started to flicker, and Mother Nature felt the arrival of the three spirits. She opened her eyes.

Above the lake floated the Spirit of the North, the Spirit of the East and the Spirit of the South. They were tall and dressed in sheer white robes through which their inner lights shone brightly. The Spirit of the North glowed indigo. The Spirit of the East blazed green. The Spirit of the South shone yellow. Mother Nature missed the red light of the Spirit of the West.

"You summoned and we came," they said with one voice. "What do you want?"

"I need your help in healing a Winged One. She is hurt badly. The claws of the Solenodon have poisoned her blood. The destruction of nature is affecting me too much, and I am too weak to heal her by myself. Unless you help, she will not survive the night."

The spirits looked at each other, but they were silent.

"Please help me," said Mother Nature. "You have been silent for too long." Mother Nature turned to the Spirit of the North. "Even you did not help Chantel on her quest in your land. Why not? What has changed?"

The spirits sighed. "We sympathize with you and are afraid of our sister, but the humans and creatures have broken their vows with us again and again. They keep hurting nature."

"But it is your sister who is hurting nature more than anyone now," cried Mother Nature. "Look at what's happening to me . . . at what's happening to our lands! Not all humans were involved, and injustice was done to the most honest creatures, the Winged Ones. Your sister killed most of them out of pure revenge, even though they were innocent. The Winged Ones were her people, the creatures under her protection. You know this! Why, it was you who helped banish her and bind her in her chains!"

The spirits responded in unison, "This is true. But after we bound our sister, we made a vow. We left the four lands to the responsibility of those who lived there. We left it up to the people and creatures there to determine their own futures, and look what they have done. It is they who have called upon the Darkness again. We have already interfered too much. And so have you, Mother Nature."

"I have no choice. With the death of every plant and animal, a piece of me dies, too. I am bound to the four lands. My life is connected to all of them. I can't let your sister, the Spirit of the West, destroy my home and my life. I have kept my oath to you. I have never revealed the truth about the Evil One, but I have fought her, and I will continue to do so. I hope you will join me and prove to me that you are not like her. At least give me some strength so that I can heal the Winged One. Correct the injustice done by your sister."

The three spirits were quiet, but Mother Nature could hear their thoughts as they discussed her plea. Finally they spoke.

"We will help you this one time. We will help you regain your strength. Walk into the lake and sit on the stone in the center. Close your eyes and wait. But this is the last time we will interfere."

"If you leave the lands and hide in your afterworld, I don't know if I can keep my oath," Mother Nature said, standing tall and strong.

"Remember what will happen to the Last Descendant if you break your oath," replied the spirits. "You know she is not ready yet to find out the truth. Continue to guide her, but do not interfere directly. This is our wisdom."

With that, the lights of the three spirits disappeared as if they had been put out by a strong wind, and they were gone.

Mother Nature did as she was told. The water in the lake started to spin. Bubbles exploded on its surface. She felt the heat from the water transfer into her body. Everything around her started to dance and turn. She kept her eyes closed and waited. The lake began to rise slowly until it covered her completely. Engulfed in the warm water, her mind traveled to distant places and old memories. She saw the young ones in the four lands play games and felt the health of nature at that time. She journeyed through endless green forests and green fields, where bright, colorful flowers grew everywhere. She knelt beside a small stream and drank its fresh water. She watched farmers harvest their crops in the fields nearby. The people were tending to the land with such love, a sight she had not seen for many, many moon crossings.

The lake slowly calmed down and settled back into its original shape and size.

Mother Nature opened her eyes and walked out of the water. Her dress was healthy again. The hundreds of leaves were moist and emerald green. She was healthy again, too. Her hair was thick and strong; her lips brilliant orange; her eyes clear and sharp.

Suddenly the cave became dark. The candles had all burnt out.

"How long was I underwater?" Mother Nature wondered.

It had only felt like a few moments, but it must have been hours. She ran through the cave as quickly as she could.

When she reached Laluna, she found her in a terrible state. Laluna's face was white, and the blanket that covered her body did not move. Laluna had stopped breathing.

CHAPTER THIRTY-FOUR

Etam Luos

Chantel, Owl, Fox and Mouse sat at the kitchen table drinking tea. Fin had gone to bed, and the remaining four were happy to spend some time together. Chantel and Mouse eagerly recounted stories about the quest. Even Fox piped up once or twice. When Chantel described her vision, Owl tapped his claws on the table.

"The person you've described reminds me of someone. He is more a legend than real," Owl said when she was finished. "His name is Etam Luos. He is the one who unites the tribes of the South, watching over them as friend and leader. He is admired for his strength, wisdom and loyalty to his people, but you will have difficulty finding him. Only he knows where he is going. He is a nomad."

"He said I would find him if I followed my heart," Chantel said. "If he lives in the South, that is where I should travel next, to find him and the Enchanted Medallion." Then she added, "Owl, what is a Soul Mate?"

Owl looked at her in surprise and took his time to answer.

"Soul Mates are the people who make us feel complete. A Soul Mate is a mate of the soul—a partner, if you may. It is a spiritual love, a love undaunted by the properties bound by this world. But why do you ask? Since the awakening of the Evil One no Soul Mates have found each other. In the past, many would meet their Soul Mates, making them feel complete, balanced."

"The Evil One spoke to me after I released the red lightning bolt," said Chantel. "She told me about Soul Mates."

"S . . . she?" Owl stammered. "You know it is a she?"

"Yes, I am sure. It's a woman's voice that speaks to me," said Chantel, surprised by this revelation. "The Evil One has been speaking to me off and on ever since I met Aquila Bellum. Now she says that our minds are connected because I released the red lightning bolt. What does that mean? Am I part of the Darkness? I don't feel like I am, but I don't know. What if she can read my mind and find out where the castle is?"

Although he looked worried, Owl said in a sure voice, "You are not part of the Darkness, Chantel. Look at how you stood up to Fin. The Evil One may be able to speak to you, but that does not mean she can read your mind."

Chantel felt much better, but she still had another worry. "The Evil One said that because I used a red lightning bolt, I freed her from one of her chains. Some Princess of Freedom I am—I am freeing our greatest enemy!"

"She may have been lying," said Owl, "or maybe not. But you needed to kill the Solenodon somehow, and if you hadn't used the lightning bolt, your friend would have died. You used the lightning bolt for good, and that means something. I wish I had all the answers, but I am not as wise as I would like to be." As Owl said this, Chantel felt her senses warning her that Owl was hiding something.

"You seem plenty wise to me," said Mouse. "Almost as wise as a Wise One!"

Owl smiled, but it looked more like a grimace.

"I wish Laluna were here now," murmured Chantel. "I wish I could tell her about the other Winged Ones."

"Winged Ones?" Owl said. "What Winged Ones? They are all dead."

"Didn't Fin tell you?" asked Chantel. "Laluna is a Winged One. You were wrong, Owl. Not only did she survive, but other Winged Ones did, too. They live with the wolves in the area between the lands of the North and the West."

"Winged Ones alive?" Owl still seemed stunned. His ears twitched nervously. "It can't be. I was told that they are all dead. I saw the burnt village myself."

"Some must have escaped. Aren't you glad?"

"Yes, yes, I am very happy, but I am shocked," Owl said hastily. "I thought they were all dead." He turned his back to Chantel. He did not know what to think. He was relieved— overjoyed—that some Winged Ones had survived. If only he could see them! But how would they feel towards him? "What shall I do?" he thought.

Fox, still thinking about the Solenodon and the lightning bolt, turned to Chantel and said in his soft voice, "I am glad you did what you did, Chantel. And I promise to stick with you no matter what happens."

"The Evil One may be able to sense you," added Mouse, "but she won't get a chance to touch you, not as long as we're around."

"Thank you," said Chantel with a big smile.

After another round of tea and some sweets, Chantel went upstairs. Her room seemed smaller, even different, but it was exactly as she had left it. Nothing had changed—nothing except herself.

She was no longer the girl who had climbed down the tree after the first night in the wild, accusing Mouse of abandoning her. She had been tempted by the Darkness and had resisted it. She had experienced pain and sorrow.

She pointed her right arm to the North, and the rune stone on her friendship bracelet started to glow. But the glow was not very bright, and it kept flickering.

After praying that Laluna would be healed quickly in Mother Nature's care, Chantel put her cloak down and made herself comfortable on the floor. She was used to sleeping on hard tree branches and needed that feeling of freedom.

"I will see you again, Laluna. Soon," Chantel whispered, as a lonely tear, shaped and shimmering like a tiny moon, slid down her cheek.

Epilogue:

Honest promises were spoken, and solemn oaths were sworn. Those who were present eighty-five moon crossings ago thought they could trust each other, but they were wrong. Everyone is susceptible to being hurt and losing themselves to the Darkness—even the Last Descendant, the Princess of Freedom.

From The Book of Erebus

End of Book One